OAKDALE

ISBN (ebook): 978-1-7376339-0-7

ISBN (paperback): 978-1-7376339-1-4

A NOVEL

KRISTI COPELAND

For my husband,
my biggest supporter.

Contents

Chapter 1   1
December 24, 2014

Chapter 2   19
December 25, 2014

Chapter 3   36
December 25, 2014

Chapter 4   49
December 26, 2014

Chapter 5   62
December 27, 2014

Chapter 6   79
December 28, 2014

Chapter 7   96
December 29, 2014

Chapter 8   108
December 30, 2014

Chapter 9   122
December 30, 2014

Chapter 10   137
December 31, 2014

Chapter 11   151
December 31, 2014

Chapter 12   168
January 1, 2015

Chapter 13   177
January 2, 2015

Chapter 14   189
January 3, 2015

Chapter 15   198
January 4, 2015

Chapter 16   207
January 5, 2015

Chapter 17   220
January 6, 2015

Chapter 18   230
January 7, 2015

Chapter 19   241
January 8, 2015

Chapter 20   253
January 9, 2015

Chapter 21   263
January 10, 2015

Chapter 22   273
January 11, 2015

Chapter 23   281
January 12, 2015

Chapter 24   292
January 12, 2015

About the Author   303
Look Out For   305

Chapter 1
DECEMBER 24, 2014

"**D**on't you have everything you have ever wanted?" Rebecca glances at Mike's reflection in the mirror and dabs at the white powder under her nose with a makeup pad, failing to be discreet.

Even though Mike can easily afford his wife's Cocaine addition, it still grates at him. Sure, a thousand-dollar bottle of Scotch is easily justified, but drugs just aren't his style. At least, not the hard stuff.

"Why would you want to change even one small detail of your superb life? I don't think a shrink will help you, at all, Michael. Especially not *Saul*." Rebecca spurts out his friend's name like it is a bitter taste on her tongue.

Something must have happened to cause Rebecca to dislike Saul, but Mike hasn't figured that out. Yet. Mike is eager to see his closest California friend, Saul Goldman. He and Rebecca met Saul and his wife

Lisette two years ago at a dolphin rescue fundraiser in Malibu; they hit it off right away. With a shared respect for fine women and Whiskey, Mike and Saul became fast friends.

Last year, after Danny died, Saul offered to meet with Mike, as a friend, not a psychiatrist. Mike passed on the offer at that time; he didn't think he needed to discuss Danny to get over his death.

Both couples look forward to the yearly Christmas Eve event held at the Friedman mansion. The $1,000-per-plate black-tie fundraiser attracts the creme de la crème. Plied with expensive champaign and the pressure of their peers watching, the attendees donate over $500,000 yearly for various college funds. It is the rare gala-goer who helps with the second part: distributing those funds to low-income families in the Los Angeles area.

Black mascara coats long, full eyelashes and Rebecca returns to swipe at her lashes for the third time. Sparkling gold powder makes her blue eyes stand out, even in the dressing room lights.

"I really wish you wouldn't do that before the party. You know I hate how you behave on that shit."

"Whatever do you mean, Michael, darling?" The squint in her eyes does not go unnoticed.

"Come on, Bec. You know what I mean. Don't you have better ways to spend my money?" The second the words fall out of his mouth, Mike cringes.

"I thought we had gotten past this," Rebecca huffs

as she turns to face her husband. "Do we seriously need to have this conversation tonight? It bores me. As you very well know, I came into this marriage with plenty of my own money. I worked my ass off for years to make my millions. Where do you get off telling me what I can and can't buy?"

"You haven't worked in a year. That makes the coke you just snorted mine." *Go big or go home*, Michael thinks to himself. *Why does it feel so good to push her buttons, lately? We've moved past the days of trying to be nice; now we just bicker.*

"Fuck you, Michael."

Mike's eyebrows raise and his chin lowers as he waits for a thorough tongue-lashing. Nothing. Rebecca rolls her eyes and turns back to the mirror and continues to primp.

That was too easy.

As much as Mike enjoys a good squabble with his wife, there is no point continuing this conversation; it's almost as old as their marriage. Mike's money versus Rebecca's money. His money not being "real" because he didn't earn it. Who has more, who came into the marriage with more, who wastes more? Good thing Mike's lawyer suggested a pre-nup.

"If you want to know the truth, I think you need to finish getting dressed, accompany me to the Friedman's fundraiser, spend a shit-ton of money on a great cause, smile, laugh, get drunk, then," a squeak of her chair brings a frown to Rebecca's flawless complexion as she stands to face her husband. "Come home and make love to your gorgeous wife. You know, the usual."

Bright red lipstick highlights plump lips as Rebecca blows Mike a kiss and raises her hand to cup his cheek, her fingernail polish is an exact match.

Lyrics from his favorite Bon Jovi song about a painted smile and blood-red nails come to mind. *Wonder how much that costs?*

"Zip me, please," Rebecca requests before she turns to face the mirror, again. Her long blonde hair is in a stylish up-do without a single strand out of place. Diamond earrings dangle from Rebecca's lobes as she finishes primping herself to perfection.

Creamy white, silky soft skin is exposed under a gold satin floor-length cocktail dress with a split that ends just below her hip. The color is a perfect match to Rebecca's shimmering La Praire eyeshadow.

Through the tension growing in his pants, Mike groans as he raises the zipper from his wife's ample hips to the nape of her long neck. The orange-blossom-and-vanilla aroma of Hermes 24 Faubourg rises to meet Mike's nose. It is unlike Rebecca to wear the 'cheap' perfume to such an event.

Teeth scrape the ridge of his wife's bare shoulder as Mike lets out a telling moan and his hands fall with gripping fingers, to her hips. Rebecca becomes wild in the sack when she's high, the only good thing about her extracurricular habit.

Before he has a chance to pull her close, Rebecca scoots away and turns toward him with a scowl. Each luscious curve is obvious under the thin dress, leaving little to the imagination. The dress exposes more skin than Mike likes. He should be the only man to see this much of his wife's body in public.

Implants from a plastic surgeon, one shared by Hollywood stars, of course, have allowed her perky C-cups to stretch the fabric to the limit. She hardly ever wears a bra, not that she needs to, and tonight is no exception.

"Do you know how long it has taken to reach this level of perfection? There is no way I am going to let you mess up one single part of this," Rebecca's hands glide up her sides, then float toward the floor.

"Aw, come on Bec. Just a quickie? I promise I won't mess up your top half." Mike winks as he takes a step forward and reaches for her. His pants grow tighter by the second.

"No!" Rebecca knits her eyebrows and swats at his hands, denying him their traditional pre-party romp. "And stop calling me that. It shows your roots."

"Well, if that didn't just ruin the mood." Mike turns toward the bed where his jacket to complete his ensemble is laid out. "Great, thanks, *Bec.*" He emphasizes the nickname to irk her.

"The mood was ruined the moment you opened your mouth, Michael."

Mike lowers himself to the footstool at the end of

the bed and leans his elbows on his knees. With coat and tie in place, he waits patiently for his bride to finish getting ready. Collar-length, usually shaggy but slicked back for the evening, his dirty blond hair is stiff with styling product. If he were being honest, Mike loathes even this level of disingenuity.

Thoughts of Danny run through his mind. The days of skipping school and stealing beers from the local grocery store in Oakdale are still known as the "good ole days". They would sneak out of Danny's basement bedroom to hang out with older kids at least once every weekend.

Twice, the group found a way to break into the high school so they could change grades in the teacher's books. Red and blue lights flashed outside the window one night while they rearranged the desks in one classroom. Small-town cops have a way of ignoring petty crime, especially when your best friend is the Police Captain's son.

"Look, Michael," Rebecca's honeyed voice interrupts his thoughts. "I know what today represents for you and I'm sorry. But it has been a year, after all. Let's go have fun tonight and drink away all of your bad memories. You need to let it go."

"It's not that easy. Rebecca. I've tried drowning my sorrows. It doesn't work."

MIKE GRASPS Rebecca's outstretched hand and assists her as she exits the limo. Cameras flash from every direction to capture images of celebrities dressed to the nines. Surely the pictures will make the cover of magazines ranging from Style to People to The Enquirer. Journalists gather and repeatedly shout questions into the air, even though no one responds.

Being married to a model has its ups and downs. On occasion, this attention is exciting, a high, almost an aphrodisiac. Tonight, it is simply annoying.

Danny is at the forefront of Mike's mind, no matter how hard he tries to shake his ghost away. It's almost as if he is standing right there, gaping at the extraordinary size of this house. Mike can almost make out the raspy *God damn, man*, his best friend's trademark phrase.

If only Mike had returned his call; if only he had known how close he was, merely three hours away. Two if he drove the Lambo. Mike closes his eyes and frowns, shaking his head to rid the sorrow. This time last year, at almost the exact time, Daniel Martin Jones was alone in a sleezy hotel room, where he decided to end his life.

What was he doing in Palm Springs, anyway?

"Michael, focus," a shrill voice brings him back to reality. Rebecca usually reserves that tone for the help.

Movie stars, Rock Gods, models, politicians, philanthropists, and top executives from L.A. and surrounding communities join their ascent of granite stairs leading to the Friedman mansion's front door.

Only six opportunities to break an ankle.

Mike giggles to himself at the visual of Rebecca falling flat on her ass.

What is wrong with me?

The usually brown trunks of Palm trees planted close to the long driveway are completely covered with strings of white lights, giving the impression that the trees are artificial. A faint Christmas melody streams from strategically placed speakers.

Rebecca's hand tightens around Mike's forearm to slow his stride. Her pace is more relaxed than most normal humans, one of many eccentricities to which Mike has grown accustomed to after their four years together. They walk side by side through the heavy wooden double doors into the foyer.

This year, the house is different.

A crystal chandelier, larger than Mike's first car, hangs from the ceiling above his head. Swirls of golden-brown emphasize the Bocote planks that line the walls of the entrance hall.

Mike is compelled to test the theory about this type of wood, so he takes two steps to the right, leans close to the wall, and inhales. The Central American wood has a slight odor of dill pickles; it must be newly installed.

Rebecca squints her eyes and shakes her head as

she lets out a long sigh, another of his wife's habits that no longer bothers Mike.

She thinks I'm crazy or maybe just common.

Poinsettias and floral holiday arrangements cover every available space on the floor and tables lining the walls. An incredibly talented designer filled blue and silver vases and planters with a mix of seasonal greens, blue Spray Roses, white Tulips, blue Gerberas, and white Spider and Fuji Mums.

Not to be outdone by his non-Jewish friends, Menorahs and Stars of David intermingle with red bows and reindeer statues.

A giant Evergreen with decorations of white and silver stands tall in the middle of the room, the Angel at the top dressed in white with clasped hands gazes down on the guests as they enter the home. She's so lifelike she could pass for a small child; Mike looks twice just to make sure she's not real.

Six chandeliers, identical to the one in the entry-way, dangle from the ceiling of the ballroom, reflecting light into every corner. A rare, white granite covers the floor of the expansive room with a black and grey mosaic of a lion in front of the stage.

This home must have cost a fortune to renovate; Mike researched the best building materials while redesigning his own home and easily recognizes and appreciates top quality.

Mike places his hand on the small of Rebecca's back to guide her into the ballroom. He wonders why she tenses at the pressure. Mike follows his wife's gaze across the ballroom directly to a stereotypical tall, dark, and handsome man.

The man that captures Rebecca's focus walks toward them in long strides, staring at Mike's wife like a wolf stalking prey. This is not someone Mike recognizes until she says his name.

"Mike, you remember Senator Benjamin?" Rebecca twists her hands in a rare anxious quirk while holding her voice steady. "Joe, you remember Mike?"

"Her husband," Mike emphasizes his title while outstretching his hand.

"Of course, Mike. Great to see you, again." The senator shakes Mike's hand without any sense of unease.

REBECCA, the queen of mingling, makes her way from model friends and their movie star husbands to the governor and his wife, then to Cher of all people. Mike glances in her direction occasionally while he visits with acquaintances.

How does she know all these people?

"Mike," Saul's arrival relaxes Mike at once. He has no idea he is tense until his friend's voice rings in his ear. "How the hell are ya?"

"Hey, Buddy." Mike turns away from an up-and-coming jazz artist, who talks about nothing more than how to properly play the saxophone, to shake Saul's hand. "Glad you made it. Took you long enough."

Saul arrives fashionably late to the fundraiser and places blame on his wife; Lisette broke a heel off her favorite pair of shoes and had a semi meltdown. He called the owner of Balenciaga and talked her into an emergency meeting at the store.

"Wow. You have the owner of a Rodeo Drive shoe store on speed dial? What is this world coming to?" Mike jokes with his friend.

Saul lets out a hardy laugh and the honest smile reaches his bright green eyes. The friends settle in cozy armchairs at the outskirts of the ballroom, uninterested in the other guests. After all, the only reason they're at this dinner is to appease their brides and to partake of the finest Whiskey in L.A. After a brief period of small talk, Mike asks the question that has held him hostage all night.

"Listen, Saul. I have a favor to ask."

"Of course, Mike. What's on your mind?"

"Not sure if you remember, but tonight is the one-year anniversary," Mike's voice trails off; he finds it difficult to find the right words and focuses on his clasped hands.

"Danny," Saul says the only word that matters.

Mike's head raises to meet kind, understanding eyes. "I need to talk it through. I miss my best friend more than I thought was possible. I can't stop thinking about when Danny and I were younger, all the shit we did to make his dad angry, and the girls we would mess around with at the Falls just south of town.

"I miss his raspy voice and the way he could shoot Whiskey like no one I have ever met. He would look a woman up and down, then tilt his head, shake it, and lick his lips before asking her out. Man, he looked like a fat man eyeing up a ribeye. All signature 'Danny' moves.

"I need to really think about who I was when Danny and I were friends. I need to understand what was going through his head. I never told you this— hell I never told anyone," Mike looks around the room to ensure no one overhears their conversation.

"Saul. He wrote me a letter. He didn't give details, but from what he said, I think he was molested. I think that lead to his death. He signed off by saying he will always love me. I never said those words to him, but I should have."

Saul nods, encouraging Mike to continue.

"I got this letter ten minutes after my mom called me to tell me that Danny died. What I don't get is what he was doing in Palm Springs. He didn't call me. Each time we planned on getting together, we would talk for a week beforehand to cement what we were going to do, with who, and when. I can't shake the feeling that he wasn't in California to see me."

"How did that make you feel?" Saul asks in true Psychiatrist fashion.

Mike lowers his voice before continuing. "I tried

all night not to break down and cry as the tears rolled down my face. I felt so cold and empty, like a lost soul out of place. Saul, I really need your help. What do I do?"

Saul takes a deep breath, leans forward, exhales, and gives his friend an honest answer from his heart. "Look, Mike. I seriously think you need to take some time and go back to Tennessee. As soon as possible. Tomorrow, even. Everyone who loves you for you is there.

"Celebrate Christmas with your mom and nephew. Since his dad is not around, I'm sure Steve would love to see you; it's been too long. Go. Find yourself and rediscover Danny. He would want you to see your family. His family."

Saul reassures Mike with his confidence. "When you come back, we'll get to the root of this, together. I will make time whenever you're ready. While you're back home, you call me if you need to talk." Saul nods at his friend and adds, "Promise me."

"I promise. But tomorrow is Christmas," Mike starts to speak but is interrupted.

"Yes, and you own a jet. You'll go tomorrow?" Eyebrows raised; Saul expects confirmation.

Mike nods and shows his friend a thankful smile.

"Good. Now, go find your beautiful bride so we can choose a vacation package to spend loads of money building. I hear island-hopping in Greece is one of the options."

Mike follows Saul's advice and stands to search for his wife. Heading for the bar, he figures she is most likely talking up one of her model friends' surgeon husbands so she can finally have her ankles "fixed," whatever that means. The ballroom is so crowded he turns sideways to move between bodies.

Unable to locate Rebecca on the main floor, Mike climbs the carpet-covered Granite steps to the second floor. Meeting rooms, a library, and a study accompany the multiple bedrooms on the upper level. In addition to living with a large family, the Friedman's conduct most of their business in this house.

Mike knows the rooms well; his first year in Los Angeles, he finalized some financial transactions with Glen Friedman. The study is the fourth door on the right, decorated with dark Dalbergia panels and furniture custom-made of trees from the same South African region.

Glen tells the tale about how this room was constructed each time Mike visits the house. On a nostalgic whim, he opens the familiar door to take a peek inside.

When Mike first sees his wife, he almost says "hey Bec," but then he recognizes the activity taking place in the Friedman study. His wife straddles Senator Benjamin on the Chaise Lounge to the left of the desk.

Mike always wondered about the purpose of this piece of furniture.

With her eyes closed and head tilted back, moaning only loud enough to be heard if you tried, Rebecca whispers her lover's name between heavy breaths.

"I love that you're wearing my favorite scent," Joe hisses and Rebecca leans forward to plant a long, wet, heavy kiss on the lips of the man beneath her.

The gold dress hangs perfectly over one leg, the other with muscles visibly flexing as she repeatedly raises herself, then lowers with a gasp. It would have been hot to watch a woman grind on the subject in this position while the man's strong fingers gripped creamy smooth skin of a perfect round ass, if this wasn't his wife.

Mike watches Rebecca fuck the Senator for what seems like an hour before he clears his throat.

The motion does not stop at Mike's initial attempt to interrupt the passion. Joe opens his eyes, realizes who is in the room, smirks, and pulls the woman down on him. Hard. Hard enough for Rebecca to cry out and move faster, moan louder.

Joe gasps and closes his eyes as Mike closes the door.

THE ROAR of the Lamborghini's engine echoes in the three-car garage as Mike backs out of the enclosure.

Red bricks separating white bricked squares pave the way to Calle De Barco.

Sharp curves keep Mike's anxiety in check until he reaches Hwy 1. Once on the highway, Mike heads north toward the Malibu Pier. Always busy, it's not the best place to be alone, so he keeps driving.

A heavy foot pushes the gas pedal to the floor and lets up only to shift gears. Blue LED lights the Speedometer as the needle reaches the nine-o-clock position; just over 100 miles per hour. Mike's heart races as he pushes just a little further. He envisions Danny sitting in the passenger seat and hears him holler "God damn, man!" At the thought, Mike smiles.

Two minutes later, he pulls a U-turn and parks on hard-packed sand beside the road at Corral Beach. Salty air reaches lungs accustomed to living near the ocean. Mike exhales and gazes out the windshield before lifting the lever on the door. The car resembles a spaceship with the doors open perpendicular to the body.

Grains of sand find their way into Mike's shiny black shoes, so he takes them off, along with his socks, and sets them beside the car; he will shake them out later. Barefoot, Mike makes his way to the edge of the water and lets the cool waves roll over his toes. Is it the ocean or tears that wet his feet?

Plopping into the sand butt-first, Mike leans forward to rest his arms on his knees. "Danny? Are you here? Dude, I can hear your voice. I can hear your laugh. I can smell the weed you just smoked. Did you save me some?"

A sound that resembles more of a hiccup than a laugh escapes Mike's throat. "Why did you do it, man? What the fuck? Wasn't there any other option?"

Tears run down Mike's cheeks as the waves of a breathing ocean break five feet from him. His head leans forward and rests on his arms as his shoulders shake from uncontrollable sobs. This is the first time Mike has really let it all out, his first honest cry for his best friend's short life.

"I'm sorry that I left you, Danny. You should have moved out here with me; maybe you would still be here if you had. You would still be alive. Dude, I miss so much about Tennessee. I want to go back so bad, but how can I after the way I left things?

"I miss you, my mom, Pops. Lisa. Man, I still wake in the night to find her on my mind. Maybe Saul is right. Maybe I should go back. I need to reconnect with the true me."

The ocean gets closer with each exhale; Mike knows it's time to go home. Not just up the hill in Malibu, but his only true home. Tennessee. Now that his mind is made up, he can't wait to set a flight plan.

Sand sticks to his feet as Mike pulls on his socks; he doesn't care. One of the scissor doors opens with an easy push of a button, allowing Mike to gracefully fall into the bucket seat.

One hour later, Mike's pilot is logging the flight plan. He will deal with Rebecca later. The most important thing in his life, at this moment, is getting home.

Home.

Chapter 2

DECEMBER 25, 2014

"Saul, hey. Yeah, sorry I left so fast." Mike calls his only true friend in California. "Look, I will explain everything later, but in a nutshell, Rebecca doesn't know that I saw her fucking Senator Benjamin in the study.

"Yeah. It sure is fucked up. I'm on my way to Tennessee, as we speak. I took your advice, Saul. Thank you. I will call you in a couple days."

The mostly one-sided conversation takes less than a minute to complete. Saul understands that Mike needs this time; after all, it was his suggestion.

The black sky fills the window as Mike tries to find something to focus on 25,000 feet below the airplane. At four in the morning, not many lights shine from the midwestern cities. The darkness in the plane and outside matches Mike's mood. He's caught up in thoughts of Danny.

Danny and Mike meeting in third grade after Danny's family moved to the area; becoming friends the day Mike offered Danny half of his sandwich at lunch; days of spending time at each other's houses, in the company of their families; Danny and Mike in high school, their lives interwoven.

Captain and Mrs. Jones kept a tight rein on their son but still allowed him to enjoy life to the fullest. Mike's parents, Mr. and Mrs. Higgenbottom, raised a different kind of family. They allowed their boys to run wild and had no rules to speak of. Blending their family values allowed both Mike and Danny to enjoy an adventurous childhood while developing high morals and good manners.

Trouble of various kinds was usually Mike's idea —Danny, his willing accomplice. When Danny came up with a new way to have fun, Mike would add some excitement and make it happen.

One brisk fall day, Danny suggested they explore the acreage adjacent to the Higgenbottom property and Mike took it a step further when he led the way into the neighbor's barn and opened the chicken and rabbit enclosures. Animals weren't meant to be caged.

The neighbor had an idea who let his animals free but could never prove it. For months, chickens and rabbits wandered through Mike's yard. Each time his mom questioned him Mike feigned innocence.

Danny and Mike shared almost everything, their toys, their money, their family—but not their girls. Amanda and Lisa had been best friends just like Danny and Mike. Senior year, when the four of them started dating, they were inseparable.

When did you start to change, Danny? How old were we when your grades started to slip? I guess you never really had good grades, did you? But I didn't either.

We both started messing around with girls when we were real young, but everyone else was, too. Weren't they? God, Danny. How could you hide this from me? We spent every waking moment together and you never said a word about someone acting inappropriately. Did you? Did I miss some signs? I wasn't even looking. How would I have known?

Was that why you had nightmares? I remember the drawings you made in our sophomore year. Black, aggressive pencil drawings of some sort of boogieman. He looked like Bigfoot to me. I thought you saw something in the woods behind my house one day. You just laughed and blew me off when I mentioned it. Was that drawing made because someone touched you?

We both did little things to get in trouble; it wasn't just you. Most of the time it was my idea and we knew your dad would cover for us. You just made it easier to get away with stupid shit. We just had fun, right? Or was that your way of acting out? Looking for help?

Danny, man, I wish you were here. I'm so sorry I couldn't be there for you. I should have called more, visited more. If you could have played for the Dodgers and been closer...yeah. I doubt that would have changed anything. I just thought we would be best friends forever. Brothers. Forever isn't over, yet. I thank God that we were able to jet around the US to get together as much as we did. Those last-minute adventures were the best.

MULTI-COLORED lights from Oak Ridge fill the space below the plane. As Mike's Beechjet 400A moves closer to the ground, the cityscape grows more colorful. Mike smirks at the memory of playing with Christmas gifts and sharing Danny's, then frowns at the thought of not having Danny by his side as he returns to visit family.

Christmas day traditions began at an early age for Mike and his big brother, Sam. They woke up hours before their parents to separate gifts into piles in front of everyone's designated chair. There was no reason to waste time moving packages around after Mom and Dad strolled into the living room. With everything organized, they could tear into the gifts immediately.

Sam taught Mike how to tell who wrapped which gifts; paper creased and taped without flaws, finished with bows and ribbon were Mom's, while Dads were wrinkled, uneven, and had names written in Sharpie.

The obvious lack of effort their dad put into wrapping presents always bothered their mom but if she complained, their dad flew off the handle in yet another overblown argument. Sam and Mike both cringed during the hour of bickering in the background while they opened presents without speaking a word. Every year, their mom whispered an apology for nagging as she walked out of the room.

After they cleaned up the room full of wrapping paper, they snuck out the back door to the barn. Their dad owned plenty of toys to ride around the property and they would choose their favorite for the day.

Mike liked the go-cart the most and Sam usually chose the four-wheeler. Unless they wanted to explore the woods, then it was a dirt bike for each of them.

As Mike watched the plane speed towards the ground, his smile faded; he could hear Dad yelling at Mom because she burned the bacon, like it was yesterday.

'God damn it, Jan. Can't you fucking figure out a simple task after ten years? It's fucking bacon.'

'Ronnie, please lower your voice. The boys...'

Although his dad always said he was just talking loudly, not yelling, his mom's tear-streaked face told a different story.

OLIVER SPRINGS AIRPORT is conveniently located just North of Oak Ridge, a mere ten miles from the house Mike bought for his mom on Melton River's edge. As Mike requested, a Lincoln Town Car waited near the tower and the driver reached for his bags as he approached.

"Merry Christmas, Mr. Higgenbottom," the limo driver smirked. "Where to, sir?"

Mike groaned at the sound of his last name. "It's Allen, now Mr. Smalls, remember? Merry Christmas to you, my friend. You're awfully chipper for 6 am, aren't you, Coach?" Mike joked with his old high-school-coach-turned-Limo-company-owner as he slid into the back seat.

"I don't think I'm ready to see my mom, yet. How about a leisurely drive around Oakdale?"

VEERING to the right off Camp Austin Road, Mike cringes at the road sign. Living at the end of Charles Brown Rd. was a popular joke during high school. How many times had he heard "Is Charlie Brown your dad?" As if a cartoon comic strip character could seriously be your dad.

Mike's childhood home, in the center of the Coal Cut Branch Forest, looks exactly as it did when he left five years ago: a ranch-style home with one window on each side of the front door; three steps leading to the entrance.

However, it appears much smaller than when he and Sam lived there together as best buds. A new coat of paint and more flowers around the house hasn't changed the structure; the bones are the same.

He steps out of the car, walks through the dusting of snow in the ditch and leans his forearms on the top rail of the fence. The Christmas-morning rising sun provides a surreal backdrop to the ranch of Mike's previous life.

Memories play in his mind like a movie starring the best friends of Mike's youth. He can almost hear the roar of the four-wheelers and smell the mixed fuel.

Three barns and multiple horse paddocks remain on the property. Even though a round bale of hay is placed strategically in the pasture to allow the animals access to fresh food, black, bay, and palomino horses graze on grass that pokes through the snow.

Multi-colored goats dot the empty spaces between the equine. The new family added two donkeys to share the responsibility of keeping the animals safe from coyotes.

A round pen and what looks like a training arena beside the horse barn is visible from the road. A brand-new trampoline is set up in the backyard and a minibike leans against the inside wall of the barn.

Kids must live here. I wonder if they have all the toys in the barn like Sam and I did. God, we would ride for hours and hours through the woods...did the property even end???

Just then it occurs to Mike that all those years they had been riding on state land, not their own property. Sam had told him that it was their land, but he either didn't know or didn't care that it wasn't. Mike would have most likely told his mom if they had strayed too far.

That explains the fence without gates that Sam broke through when we first got dirt bikes.

A smirk forms on Mike's lips as it all makes sense. The trails he and Sam carved out with their toys and the deer they hunted each season belonged to the fine state of Tennessee, not the Higgenbottom's. Mom would have made her boys stay on their own property, but Dad wouldn't care.

As Coach opens the back door for his fare, Mike nods to the front door of the Lincoln and asks Coach if he minds driving a customer in the front seat.

"I thought you'd never ask." Coach Smalls replies with an ear-to-ear grin. "I have to say, Mike, you've been pretty quiet. The drive from the airport was not what I expected from my best player. After five years, I thought you would have more to say."

Coach could always read Mike like a book; he sensed when his favorite players had bad days when no one else noticed. Between classes, Coach would pull Mike into his office and ask if he wanted to talk about it. Gaining respect from his players had been important at the time, but Coach hadn't realized how close a select few would become. Mike and Danny, for instance.

"Coach, I'm sorry. I'm really just trying to figure

shit out. Being gone for so long and spending time with people who only know Mike Allen, I guess I forgot how much you already know about my life." Flashing a smile at his friend, Mike continues. "I have to say that I totally forgot what a genuine southern accent sounds like. I have worked really hard to lose my roots in California."

Changing the subject, Mike asks, "I haven't even asked about you. I apologize. How are you? How is Mrs. Smalls? Is she missing you today? It's Christmas Day after all. You should be with her not toting me around the countryside."

"Oh, Higgs, we're just fine, thanks." Glancing at Mike, Coach chuckles at the eye-roll. The nickname from high school makes Mike shake his head. "Yes, it is Christmas, but the wife and I spend every day together. We celebrated our Christmas last night because you called for today. She sends her love.

"You know I haven't coached since you and Danny graduated. I had to do something with my time, so I started a driving business. The Mrs. is still giving Piano lessons and just loves the kids she teaches. Still has that giant heart.

"Changes in Oakdale aren't usually big, Mike, you already know that. Except for you, that is. You have been the talk of this town since the day you left. For the first couple of years, everyone was jealous. Now word is that money can't buy happiness."

Mike expects to sense tension from Coach's

comment. Instead, compassion fills the cab of the limo. "Hey, Coach? Could you take me down to Dale Road?"

Mike ran over this scenario a thousand times in the past 12 hours. A million or more in the past year. How does he not completely break down when he stands in Danny's driveway?

"Danny's parents moved, you know. Too many memories." Coach catches Mike's eye.

"They did? I didn't know that. Makes sense. I really want to see the house, anyway, if you don't mind."

Coach nods and turns east.

"Where do they live, now? Are they still in Oakdale?"

"No. They moved to a really nice place in Herriman on the golf course. Danny left them a ton of money when he died, however, I'm not sure how he was able to save that much. I heard from them last year when his parents hired me to drive them to an upscale Halloween party. Linda told me that Danny wanted to be sure they were taken care of for the rest of their lives."

Once they reach the old Jones house, a heaviness overwhelms Mike. He hesitates for a minute before the door opens. Coach stands outside with an outstretched hand. The leather on his glove squeaks as Mike grips him for help.

As Mike closes his eyes, the cold of the day disappears, his worldview much smaller, his heart larger. Danny's wearing shorts and a tank top in Mike's memory; new Nike Air Zoom's shine bright in the summer sun. Danny laughs as he bounces a basketball and sinks a three-pointer. *Swish.* Then his friend turns to greet him. *'Higgs, man, what's up?'*

The sound of Danny's voice is so real that Mike opens his eyes expecting to see him standing by his side. Instead, the old two-story house stands empty, a bright mockery. He doesn't realize he is crying until Coach asks if he's okay and hands him a handkerchief.

"Shit, Coach. I can't do this, today. I really thought I could but..." Mike wipes the tears and sniffles as his voice trailed off. The door of the Town Car opens and Mike slides into the warm cabin.

"WHAT WERE you and Danny thinking that night y'all broke into this place to change your grades? I know that wasn't your first time. You're just lucky it was me that caught you."

Mike's laugh echoes between the walls of the U-shaped building where the high school students bring their lunch to eat on nice days. "We weren't, Coach. That's the thing. That's what made it fun. It wasn't our first time and, no, it wasn't our last." The friends continue their walk around the building to the north side of the school.

Mike smiles and turns in a circle to take in the entire view of the high school and the parking lot where he and Danny did donuts every chance they got. Memories of skipping school and sneaking in late to class play at his mind.

"You would think that out of 150 kids in the school, they would be able to figure out who the good kids were versus the delinquents. God, we were such little rats. We did some stupid shit, but none of it was really that bad, was it?

"Of course, Danny's dad was Captain the entire time we were in school. He caught us that last time. We weren't changing grades then, though, we were just bored. Captain Jones begged us to find some other activity to keep us occupied.

"That's when we started going to the overlook and bonfire parties in the Kicker's parent's extra cow pasture. A different kind of trouble, a different kind of fun. I don't even remember his name, how bad is that? Chad something?

"Danny and I met up with Amanda and Lisa Senior year after a bonfire. We took the girls to the overlook for some drinks and the rest is history." Mike sits on the cold brick half-wall under an over-hang. "This place. God, Coach, so much has changed. Everything has changed."

"It sure has, Mike. You know, I knew you kids did

a lot of drinking and thanked God every Monday when everyone showed up for practice before class. These mountain roads are so dangerous on a good day, let alone when y'all got drunk.

"Captain Jones and I had extra eyes on the entire class, especially when y'all got crazy. I picked up a couple of your classmates multiple times to keep them off the roads.

"Lisa was always such a good girl. She was so good for you, Danny, too. She and Amanda kept the two of you out of real trouble, didn't they?"

"Yeah," Mike let out a quiet laugh. "Man, I miss her, Coach. She truly is the one that got away. If I wouldn't have been a drunk working at Red's, she might have gone with me to California. She might be my wife instead of the shallow, selfish rich witch in L.A."

~

"I USED TO LOVE THIS PLACE." Butter and garlic scent the air and as Mike inhales, his stomach growls. Roane St. Grille in Harriman has the best southern comfort food around. He and Coach find a booth and a perky waitress hands them menus.

"So, Mike, tell me. What's it like to have an unlimited amount of money? You can buy anything; is it as satisfying as you thought it would be?"

Mike knows better than to take offense at an old

friend's direct questions. Coach truly wants to understand Mike's state of mind. "In a nutshell, it's freaking great to not have to worry about what things cost. Above and beyond that though, to be honest, the physical things that I have—the house and cars—aren't making me happy. Not anymore. The plane, though, that's a sweet perk.

"For a long time, it was better than any dream I could have had. Once you get into that lifestyle and meet the people who are in a similar situation, it's surreal. Coming from new money makes you different than those who grew up with money, though.

"For about a year, I just threw my status around, paid cash for any extravagant thing I could find. Jewelry, cars, art, furniture. After I met Rebecca, I had to tone it down, had to buy some clothes, change my name, and lose the accent. As she always says, I had to hide my roots."

"I'm sorry to hear that, Mike. I thought you were proud to be from Oakdale. Is it that hard to fit in with other people? Just because they're rich, you had to change who you are? That hardly seems fair."

"Yeah, it's a totally different world, Coach."

The young waitress bounces to their table delivering cokes and takes their order, a Chicken Fried Steak meal for Mike and a Catfish basket for Coach.

"So, how's business, Mike? What is it you do, again? Something with musical groups? How did you get into that line of work?"

"I had to do something to keep me busy. When I managed Red's, I was in my element. I knew I drank too much, which I blame for ruining a very special relationship, so I quit drinking while I worked.

"When I bought my first bar, it had a stage, and I had an epiphany. We always had to travel so far to hear good music, so I brought music to my customers. Good music. I named the place after my friend who made it all possible. Gene, God rest his soul, left me his entire estate. I digress…

"I didn't book huge names, I promoted up and coming stars. After Gene's got so busy and I could hardly keep up, I opened Lisa's; then came Sam's. Obviously named for the most important people in my life.

"I will have you know that *Heaven Scent* played at Lisa's for three months before they got a record deal. Ah, you probably haven't heard of them, though. They're a small-town girl band from Michigan that came to L.A. looking to make it big. Well, they did.

"Six months ago, I went in a different direction and opened a sports bar complete with multiple sixty-inch TVs on every wall. The General Manager books all kinds of athletes to come in and spend time with underprivileged kids in the area. He's an ex-football player and a really great guy. Can you guess what I named that bar?" Mike raises an eyebrow at his friend.

"Coach's?"

Mike nods, a playful smile at his lip.

"Really, Mike? That's so cool. I'm honored," Coach can hardly contain his pleasure; his smile radiates. "What about your wife? You've mentioned Rebecca. How did y'all meet? What's her story?"

"Gosh, Coach, I'm talking your ear off. Are you sure I'm not boring you?"

"Hey, I asked. Come on, Mike. This is the most excitement I've had in a year. Talk, son."

"Okay, okay. Here's the short version. I met Rebecca at one of the first big expensive parties that I attended. I was a mess, all awkward and underdressed. She was a model for the Auto Show at the time. Gorgeous. Oh, my God, Coach, if you saw her." Mike's smile fades as the memory of his first impression of his wife gives way to the current situation.

"I never really loved her, even though she made me say it. Honestly, Coach, she was just a tweener." Coach squints and shakes his head, so Mike elaborates, "you know, someone in between two people who really matter.

"I've known all along that she wasn't 'the one'. I asked her to marry me after dating for only six weeks. We both needed a partner, you know, someone to accompany each other at parties and fundraisers. It felt like the right time." As Mike talks about Rebecca, he can't hide his disappointment from Coach.

"Ugh, Rebecca. I really should call her. She's left me eight messages and has probably called the police. Or not. Who knows?" Mike puts his head in his hands and can feel his friend staring at him.

Once he looks up, Coach agrees, "Yeah, you really should call."

THE NEW JONES' home backs up to the eighth hole of the Emory Gold and Country Club, a mile west of Herriman. A beautiful 4,000-square-foot house stares back at Mike as he sits in the Town Car. An unusual feeling of peace settles on his shoulders. Danny knows his parents are doing just fine.

With a heavy heart, Coach says, "Mike, you know I'm not good at this kind of thing. I'm awful sorry about Danny; I know he was more than just your best friend. He was your family. I'll wait out here if you want to go say hello."

"Thanks, Coach. I really thought I was ready for this conversation, but I think I need more time to think it through. I'll come back another day. Besides, I should at least bring flowers for Mrs. Jones. Would you please take me to my mom's now?"

Chapter 3
DECEMBER 25, 2014

F lour dusts the ceramic rolling pin reducing the sound of the clank with each push and pull on the soon-to-be buttermilk biscuits. Jan Higgenbottom brushes the fly-away strands of blonde hair from her eye with the back of her hand hoping a stray hair doesn't fall into the dough.

"Jingle Bells" chimes from the doorbell and startles Jan. She lets out a huff as she walks out of the kitchen. The Santa Clause apron was clean before she wipes her hands on the front, smudging Santa's nose.

Who would be at the front door on Christmas Day? Doesn't everyone have some place to be?

As Jan walks down the hall, she forces the frown off her face; it is Christmas after all.

SHRUBS DECORATED with white Christmas lights line the sidewalk of the two-story brick home. Faux flames flicker in each window carrying on a beloved family tradition. Plastic smiles of Angels, Reindeer, and Elves greet Mike on the front stoop. His heart seems to grow two sizes at the sight as if he were previously the Grinch.

Five years ago, two weeks after his inheritance was deposited into his bank account, Mike signed closing documents on this house. Three weeks later, Jan moved a few of her belongings from Oakdale. Mike opened an account at a local furniture store and paid for all the items needed to live comfortably in this home.

Mike hesitates as his outstretched hand reaches for the doorbell; his head shakes with regret as he presses the button. Even though this beautiful home is his mother's residence, this is the first time he has physically been to this location; the purchase had all been completed sight-unseen.

I should have come back, earlier. How stupid to harbor feelings that kept me away from my family. What I wouldn't give to be able to just open the door, walk in, and say, "Hey, mom!"

Warm air scented with buttermilk moves Mike's dirty blond hair out of his face as the door opens. An instant feeling of home washes over his soul, bringing a genuine smile to his lips.

With open arms, Mike greets his mother. "Merry Christmas, Mom."

"Michael! Oh, my dear, what a pleasant surprise. Merry Christmas." Jan stands on tiptoes as she wraps her arms around her son's neck and kisses his cheek. Strong arms envelop Jan like only a son's gentle strength can. The embrace lasts long enough for her nose to chill.

Jan's heart swells: her son is home.

Taking a step back, Jan grasps her son's hands and widens her view. "Let me get a look at you. Oh, it's been too long, Mike. Come in, come in. I was just putting biscuits in the oven." She pulls her son into the foyer and closes the door.

"You look great, Mom. Really great. I've missed you." Beneath the apron, Jan wears a red silk button-up shirt with black slacks and black slippers. Her hair is pulled back in a bun with just her bangs loose. Flawless skin glows with a hint of pink at her cheeks.

Mike follows his slender mother through a bright, grand foyer with entrances to oversized rooms at each side. The gourmet kitchen at the end of a short hall is surprisingly clean for Jan's baking. For the second time that day, he sighs into the comforting smell of southern cooking; biscuits are cooling on the counter, buttery and warm, and another batch awaits the oven.

Visions of his dad complaining about burnt biscuits and bacon fill Mike's mind. "Mom, you can cook?"

"Why do you sound so surprised? I have always been able to cook. Maybe not to your father's standards," her voice trails off and she changes gears. Jan places another round of biscuits on a cookie sheet and slides them into the oven.

Mike fidgets, worried he offended her. "Well, they smell great. Am I interrupting, though? Do you have company coming over?"

"Of course, you're not interrupting. I'm just cooking to cook. I always make dinner for four and if anyone decides they want food, it's here. If not when it's hot, then it will be in the fridge waiting for someone to stick it in the micro."

"Well, then. It looks like I showed up at the right time. What else are you making?"

"Fried chicken is keeping warm in the microwave."

"Wow, Mom. This is surreal." Mike pulls out a barstool from under the raised countertop and sits. "You cleaned up after making fried chicken and while you made biscuits. Who are you and what have you done with my mother?" Jan blushes like a schoolgirl at the compliment.

After she sets the timer, Jan glides into the family room. Mike follows and removes two small boxes from his overcoat pocket and sets them under the ten-foot-tall Christmas tree.

"Let me take your coat. Tell me what's on your mind. What's wrong, Mike?"

"What do you mean 'what's wrong'? Can't a guy surprise his mom on Christmas Day?"

"Well, sure, dear. But not you," Jan gasps and places her hand over her heart before asking, "are you in trouble? Oh, Michael. How can I help you?"

"Mom," Mike lets out a deep laugh as he eases into an oversized chair opposite his mother in a wing-back chair that does not appear comfortable.

With crossed legs and squinted eyes, Jan confronts her son. "You must be in some sort of trouble to come home after all this time. You didn't come back when your brother lost everything, when your dad got married, when your best friend died. So, I'm confused; why now? And where's that wife of yours?"

"Slow down, Mom. One thing at a time," Mike runs his fingers through his mussed hair and leans forward setting his forearms on his knees. "I'm really sorry I haven't come home before now. I guess I wasn't ready. But here I am and it's Christmas. You're sure I'm not intruding?" He doesn't answer the question about his wife.

"Don't be silly," Jan brushes the thought away with a wave of her hand as she leans back letting the chair surround her. "You are always welcome in my home. Your timing is perfect, actually. Stevie is out at a friend's house for a Christmas party, so we have some time to ourselves. Well, until eleven, anyway. I am just so thrilled to see you. What a fantastic surprise.

"Oh, where are my manners. What can I get you to drink, Mike?" Jan floats into the kitchen as she tosses suggestions over her shoulder. "A beer? Wine? Coffee? Tea?"

"I would love a glass of red wine, Mom, thanks." Mike and Coach had a great day of catching up and his mom deserves to know exactly what brought him here, but he needs to recharge his batteries before going down that road.

His mom's way of asking all the pertinent questions will certainly pull more energy out of him than most people.

I need to tell her that she was right; I probably made a huge mistake moving to California. I need to figure out what this life is all about, find myself, really. Later, though.

CHICKEN BONES SIT in the middle of a square white plate and Mike's cloth napkin covers them. Jan watches, satisfied, as her son leans back in the straight-back dining room chair and places his hand on his stomach. With a groan, Mike closes his eyes. "I'm stuffed."

Peering from a slit between eyelids, he takes in his mother's toothy smile. "Mom, your cooking skills have drastically improved. That was seriously the best meal I have had in five years."

"Well, I suppose the training I completed under Mrs. Dean proves to be effective."

"Mrs. Dean?" Mike furrows his brows and shakes his head.

"Paula, dear. I spent a month in Savannah last spring and attended her cooking school. Didn't I tell you?"

"Maybe, but I don't remember. Well, Thank you, Paula." Mike stands and clears the table, placing the dishes in the sink. As he starts to rinse them, Jan asks him to stop.

"My housekeeper, Rosie, will get these in the morning, dear. Let's fill our glasses; I want to give you the official tour."

"THE HOUSE IS BEAUTIFUL, Mom. I love how you've decorated. I'm so pleased that you enjoy living here." Mike and Jan settle into comfortable furniture in the Living Room. Art depicting county landscape scenes tastefully decorates the spacious area.

"Well, it's a little bigger than I need, but with Stevie, it feels full. He brings so much action to our lives that it feels like we live in a house the size of Oakdale.

"And Rosie stays here full-time, I told you about her. She's more than a housekeeper; she's become a close friend. We keep each other company and we both feel safer with this arrangement. I didn't take you into her rooms. She has her own en suite, half kitchen, and a living room. The house fits us all just perfectly."

"That's great, mom. I'm really glad you feel comfortable. I thought this home may be a little too big, but the location couldn't be any better. This neighborhood is known for its safety and close-knit community.

"I can hardly imagine how our old house compares to this. How did we even live so close together?" Memories of the four Higgenbottom's practically stepping on each other as they crowded the kitchen flood back.

"It was a challenge." Jan's somber voice snaps him back to reality.

"Look, I have to be honest, besides coming to see you, I was hoping we could figure out what to do with Stevie. He's giving you fits, mom. How can I help you? How can I help him? I realize he may not want my help, but I feel like I need to do something that will ease his load. The poor kid deserves to be happy, not abandoned by every male role model he's ever had."

"Yes, Mike. He needs your help, even though he might not know it yet."

"You've told me a little about what's been happening, but I would like to know more. Sure, he's skipped a little school and stayed out too late, but what thirteen-year-old boy hasn't done that? I know Sam and I probably kept you awake way too many nights." Mike stares into his mother's eyes with empathy.

"You remember Ms. Johnson?" Jan raises one eyebrow and grins. "Of course, you do." Mike's honest smile answers the rhetorical question.

Lisa's still here. Thank God.

"Well, she's Stevie's Geography teacher and to be honest, she is the only one who acts like she cares. His other teachers just say he's simply being a boy, but Lisa has kept in constant contact with me about what she observes and how his actions have affected him.

"She knows his family history and is concerned that he may be hanging around the wrong group. With Sam turning to drugs and alcohol, we are all worried that Stevie might follow in his father's footsteps."

"Mom. He hasn't started doing drugs, has he?" Sitting straighter in his chair, Mike's shoulders tense.

"There's no absolute indication of that. Lisa has been very helpful by letting me know the signs and asking that I pay close attention. So far, I haven't noticed glassy eyes or smelled anything other than cigarette smoke.

"I was hoping that you could connect with him and share some of your experiences growing up. Coming from me, it just sounds like an old lady trying to be pushy."

"I will do more than just have a talk with him. I promise I will do my best to be that strong positive influence that he needs. I will make you proud, mom." Mike vows to never allow his nephew to follow in his father's footsteps. Jan's previous disappointments with her oldest son is more than one person should have to endure.

When Sam became addicted to heroin and lost everything he owned, Jan spent all of her time trying to get her oldest son into rehab or mental health program. He resisted to the point of severing all ties and refused to accept any form of help from his mother.

For years, Jan blamed herself for not doing enough, even though there was nothing left for her to do. She attended Al-Anon and Nar-Anon meetings to better understand the actions of an alcoholic and addict. To her surprise, she ended up learning more about herself and why she felt the need to fix her son.

All these years later, she still had nightmares about Sam being abused by her brother, the town preacher. Jan asked for Ronnie's help, but he just acted like nothing was wrong and brushed the entire conversation under the rug.

The day Jan found Stevie sleeping on a cardboard box next to his dad behind the Home Depot was the last day she set eyes on Sam. Disgusted at herself for not being able to help and angry with her son for endangering the life of her only grandchild, Jan took Stevie home and gave him everything he needs to be a good teenage boy.

The only man left in Stevie's life lives a thousand miles away. It is about time Mike came home; Stevie needs him more now than ever.

"Together, we will guide him in the opposite direction than Sam took," Mike reassures his mother.

Jan reaches out to her son and touches his hand. "Thank you for coming home. I don't know how long you intend to be here, but please stay as long as you need." Blue eyes shine with joy.

"I want to hear all about Pops. How is the old spit-fire?" Mike laughs as he changes the direction of the conversation to break up the emotion.

"Your Grandpa is doing well. He's living at Canterfield, just five miles away. The assisted living community has been just fantastic for him. He has friends that he plays games with and if he needs someone to talk to, professionally, they are just a building away. You know, his PTSD still flares up every now and then, but the therapist on site has worked wonders with him."

"Canterfield? Why does that name sound familiar?" Mike rubs at the scruff on his chin. "Is that the place Lisa's Grandmother lived?"

Jan nods.

"I visited her with Lisa a couple times after high school. If it's anything like it was then, I'm sure Pops is in good hands. That's great that they have therapists there for PTSD; I worry about him still having episodes. I have really missed him a lot, Mom. I'm going to go see him as soon as I can. When should I visit?"

"Oh, I usually go see him on Fridays. He has appointments and activities to fill almost every day. He's a wiz at the Trivia and sometimes I go early to watch him win. Most weeks, though, I arrive around 3:30 pm. That seems to be a good time for him."

"Tomorrow's Friday. Do you mind if I tag along?"

"Of course not."

Mike clears his throat and gazes over his mother's shoulder before he gathers enough courage to ask about his brother. "Where is Sam, mom?"

"Oh, Mikey," Jan shakes her head and stares at her clasped hands. "I can barely stand to think about how he lives. Last I knew, he was in a camp with a bunch of other people over behind the Home Depot. They all live in tents set up on the edge of the woods and share a bonfire and whatever food they can find. They literally eat from hand to mouth while the rich drink from a golden cup.

"It still bothers me that he wouldn't accept any help from either of us. He's so proud; he wants his own money, well, that isn't working so great, now. I appreciate everything you have done for me, but still feel horrible that we all live so well and Sam...doesn't."

Jan swipes a tear away as she turns her head, clearing her throat as she stands. "Well, it's late and you're tired. Let's talk more tomorrow."

STILL TOO WORKED up to lie down, Mike fills his glass and sits at the table in the breakfast nook.

Merry Christmas, Danny. It's been a long day. Did you get everything that happened? There are so many things to do, so many people to see. I can't wait to see Pops and I plan on visiting your parents as soon as I can.

Stevie needs my attention most, though. I'm hoping you can give me some strength—help guide me to do the right thing, say the words he needs to hear. I miss you, man.

A faint click cuts through his thoughts and Mike turns his head toward the door leading to the Garage. Light glows from the stainless-steel Rolex on Mike's left wrist; 10:55 pm. He nods his head in approval.

At least he respects curfew. He hasn't turned into a total troll. We can work with this, Danny.

Stevie strolls past the kitchen but doesn't notice his uncle sitting in the dark. Mike prefers that he talk to his nephew in the morning after everyone has had time to rest. Taking one night of worry from his mother was the goal for tonight.

Chapter 4
DECEMBER 26, 2014

"I brought you a Christmas gift, Mom." Mike places a small box in front of his mother on the table where she sits in the breakfast nook. Rosie clears the plates and takes them to the kitchen as Mike and Jan continue their conversation.

"Oh, Mike. I didn't get anything for you." Jan reaches for the box and lifts it to her ear giving it a little shake. A smile graces her lips as she giggles at the ritual. She taught her sons to shake every wrapped gift to make sure it wasn't a prank, like a cat wrapped in a box, as her brother gave her one year for her birthday.

"Oh, dear. You have outdone yourself. This is too much," Jan lifts the stainless-steel Ballon Bleu de Cartier watch from the box and rethinks her statement. With a slight shake of her head, she changes her mind. "Wait. What am I saying? Scratch that.

Thank you, Michael. This is beautiful, I love it. And I love you. I am so happy you're here."

"I love you, too, Mom. Now that I am here, my path in the universe seems a little clearer." Mike takes a deep breath and exhales in preparation for a deep declaration. Jan rests her chin in her hand as she listens to her son's bass voice explain the true reason why he came home.

"I've been wandering, Mom. I've known it for a while but didn't know what to do. You, this trip, this house, this town, has brought clarity. I know I made a huge mistake moving to California. At the time, I thought I was going to change my life and become a superstar. I had all this money and no idea how to handle it.

"I know y'all said I was moving too fast and that I would regret it, but it seems that it took five years and a few million dollars to figure that out. My life did change, but not nearly the way I envisioned. The time I spent away from Oakdale has been a great learning experience and I am very thankful for the opportunities that the inheritance provided. May Gene rest in peace.

"Being away from the ones who love me most, who I love most has been harder than I thought it would be. When you first called about Stevie in September, I truly thought the entire situation would work itself out, but now I realize that I am needed here. In short, I know you love to hear these words: You were right, Mom."

With a sigh and a smile, Jan nods. Not one to say I told you so, she reaches for Mike's hand, clasps it with her own, and offers to make more coffee.

"HEY, SLEEPYHEAD."

Arms and legs pause in mid-stride as Stevie stops in his tracks before he turns his head towards the breakfast nook. Based on pictures Stevie had seen of the golden mime statues on the pier in San Francisco, he thought this awkward stance must make him look like one. After he repositions himself, Stevie lifts a hand to smooth his medium-length, black hair that sticks out at all angles.

"Um, hey." With a glance at his grandmother, Stevie knits his eyebrows and tilts his head. Could his uncle Mike seriously be sitting in his house? Jan nods in the direction of Mike and puts the plate of leftover breakfast in the microwave.

Leaning back in his chair, Mike lifts his chin in greeting. "Merry Christmas, Bud. How the heck are ya?"

"I'm fine, why?" Stevie pulls out a stool and sits at the bar with his back to his uncle.

Moving from the breakfast nook, Mike sits on the

stool next to Stevie. "Just making small talk. Man, you got big."

"Yeah, from my vast experience, people grow from birth until about the age of seventeen. Five years of growth is pretty obvious when you're not around to see it."

Mike lets out a gruff chuckle and pats his nephew's shoulder. "Good one, Bud. Your grandma said you were out at a Christmas party last night. Did you have fun?"

"Sure."

"You know, when I was your age, your grandma wouldn't have let me go to a party. She must be getting soft in her old age."

"Michael!" Jan turns and sticks out her tongue.

"I'm glad she's letting loose of the reins a little. Good for you; go have fun."

"Um, I did." Stevie stares at Mike for five whole seconds before asking: "Grandma what's for breakfast?"

I guess I deserved that. Stings a little, though, not being able to have a conversation with my own nephew. This may be harder than I thought.

"Here. I brought this for you. Merry Christmas, Stevie." Mike places a box wrapped with Santa paper in front of his nephew and follows his eyes from the microwave to the gift back to the back of his grandmother's head.

"Look, I know I haven't been home for a really

long time, but that has nothing to do with you. I needed the time away and I'm afraid I took too long. I was selfish and I'm sorry. Will you please accept my apology and open your gift?"

With pursed lips, Stevie looks at the gift and back at his uncle. His eyes soften and the corner of his lips turn up in a slight smile.

"Go ahead, I think you'll like it." Mike nudges the package an inch closer to Stevie.

Santa's hat rips in half as the paper falls to the counter revealing a box holding a miniature video camera. "Seriously? A GoPro HERO? I've been saving my allowance for one of these. Dude, this is sweet!" Stevie's grin widens to a full-out smile.

Stevie turns to his uncle and puts his arms around his neck; Mike releases a long breath and pulls him close.

Jan smiles to herself and turns to look out the window; a small hiccup sound escapes her throat. The GoPro HERO is the ice breaker Mike needs to get through his nephew's tough exterior. "Thanks, Uncle Mike. I love it."

"DANNY and I used to spend most of our time in the woods with your dad. Grandma and Grandpa had the best toys: four-wheelers, dirt bikes, snowmobiles, horses, you name it."

"Horses?"

"Yeah. One time, when your grandpa was out of gas and we wanted to get away from the house, we saddled up three of your grandma's old geldings and took off into the woods. They are a way different kind of fun. Riding a machine, open throttle, that you can totally control is great, but have you ever had to communicate with an animal with your arms, legs, and energy? It's amazing."

"No, but I've never really been on any of the machines, either."

"Mom? Why have you been depriving my nephew of the most fun a kid can have?" Mike gazes at Jan with raised eyebrows; his mother shakes her head.

"So what activity were you planning to video when you saved enough for a Go Pro?" What else is there besides fast machines, animals, and cars?

"Chase and a couple other guys have them attached to their helmets and record us while we go out on the mountain trails on our bikes. They're really fun to watch after we get back. Totally different perspective." Stevie's eyes flicker with pride.

"I can't wait to see some of your videos. If you like riding fast, I need to introduce you to Yamaha, the best off-road machines ever made. Your Grandpa Ronnie always had something that would run, but he knew his boys would ruin whatever we threw our leg over, so the toys were always used. He was right, you know. Your dad and I crashed everything but the horses."

Stevie relaxes with each story Mike recites. After he devours his breakfast, he asks more about growing up in Oakdale. "Where did y'all go when you went off on your adventures?"

"Well, most of the time we just rode around our forty acres, but when we got really froggy, we would venture up into the hills, as we called them. Our land bordered Lone Mountain, so we had almost four-thousand wild acres to roam. We loved Coyote Point the most, but we only saw a coyote there once. Scared the shit out of us and we didn't go back for years."

"Will you take me there? I haven't been anywhere cool in a long time. No offense, Grandma." Stevie shot Jan a sincere smile.

"None taken, sweetie. I know hanging out with an old lady isn't cool. Your Uncle Mike will be able to show you some super cool stuff, I'm sure."

ALLEN MCKAY SETS his paintbrush down and stares longingly at the portrait of the brunette with blue eyes that gazes over his shoulder. The one vision he was never able to erase with drugs or alcohol was that of his beloved Anna. Most Fridays during art class, he paints another picture of the only person to whom he was never able to express his regret.

The mother of his children had every right to leave and start a new life, a better life, with their children, Dominic and Jan. In 1963, most women accepted that their husbands would stray, but Anna McKay's morals wouldn't allow her to put up with any sort of betrayal from her husband. She took their marital vows seriously and expected the father of her children to do the same.

"Al, you have visitors," the raspy voice of his favorite caregiver, Miguel, brings him back to 2014. "Look who came with Jan and Stevie, today."

Allen almost can't believe his eyes; his grandson, Mike, stands between his daughter and great-grandson. The same shaggy-headed kid that left in such a hurry five years ago smiles his signature toothy grin as he leans in for a tight hug.

"Pops, you look great. How've you been?" The distinct scent of Ben Gay tickles Mike's nostrils.

"I look great? Why you kissing my ass, son? I look old and we both know it." Allen gives Mike a tight squeeze before pushing him away. "You look old, too. Where the hell ya been?"

"L.A. Five years living fast will age you, let me tell ya." Mike peers around Allen to study the portrait of his grandmother. "Hey, Pops, that painting is incredible. I remember Grandma looking exactly like that. Wow. How'd you get so good with a brush?"

Allen waves off the compliment with his hand and

a shrug. "Eh. Sit. Make yourselves comfortable. Can Miguel bring you a drink?"

"How many times do I have to tell you that I'm not your personal butler, Mr. McKay? I am not here to wait on you hand and foot." Miguel turns to the visitors and asks if he can bring them something to drink.

"Nice, Pops. You got all these people to do whatever you want. You're living better than me." Mike chuckles and nods his approval.

"I WAS the best shooter on the Rifle team, got the medals to prove it." Allen loves how his great-grandson looks at him when he tells his stories about being in the service. It warms his heart to see Stevie's eyes open wide and his mouth drop like he can't believe what he's hearing.

"The men on my team traveled all over the southwest for competitions; we placed first or second every time. We must have beaten 200 other rifle teams. We never had to wear our dress uniform anywhere because we were always on our way to or from the range or a competition. All the other guys at Fort Sam Houston spent most of their time doing chores or running around like a herd of cows.

"My team got special treatment, which was just fine with me. That all changed real quick, though."

Allen's voice trails off and he stares into the space between Jan and Stevie. He's back in 'Nam for a moment, surrounded by his eleven-man platoon, crawling through jungles and fighting a losing war on a foreign shore.

"Gramps? Tell me about when it changed," Stevie asks a second time. He wants to hear every experience that the one consistent man in his life has to tell.

"No!" Allen startles back to reality and glances at his twisted fists that sit in his lap. He clears his throat before changing directions, understanding that Stevie is still too young to hear details of the war. "Enough about my old life; that's all history. I want to know how your business is going, Mikey. Don't your stores miss you when you're gone?"

Before he responds, Mike glances at Stevie to gauge his mindset; a little deflated, but not hurt. He surely has seen this side of Allen before.

"Nah, that's the beautiful thing about owing the bars, I have fantastic General Managers. Business is great, Pops. I have four locations around L.A.; three of them focus on finding the next big star. I opened one sports bar just to shake things up a little. I spend most of my time hanging out with famous people, driving fast cars, and collecting money. Stevie, have you ever heard of Heaven Scent? They're a girl band..."

Stevie finishes his uncle's sentence: "from a small

town in Michigan. Yeah, they're great. My friends all think they're hot."

Satisfied that Mike was able to bring his nephew out of his short funk, he nods and smiles at Jan.

"Wait," Stevie sits at the edge of his chair. "You discovered Heaven Sent? That's so frickin' cool, Uncle Mike. Do you know them? What are they like? I bet they're real down to Earth, aren't they?"

"Yeah, Bud. They are."

Allen relaxes in his chair; his family's voices lull him to a light slumber. When he wakes, he is laying in his bed not sure how he got there. Mike coming home from L.A. would be terrific for Jan; after all, she talks about that boy non-stop. She's so proud. Allen hopes it wasn't just a dream.

"HOW'S DAD?" Although apprehensive about seeing his father, Mike sincerely wants to know that he is well. Before Mike left, he bought a luxury car dealership for Ronnie, but the transaction took place without Mike present. Their relationship had been rocky since he was fifteen. Mike witnessed his dad push his mom to the floor during one of their arguments making her cry. Again.

Things were never quite the same. After that day, Mike couldn't look at his dad with the respect he once had. Sam told him he had seen something similar a few weeks prior; the realization that his dad was a big-time jerk changed how Mike viewed his world. The small town of Oakdale revered Ronnie Higgenbottom for his volunteer work within the community, but Mike knew it was all for show.

He heard his dad mention that the folks in their town were all suckers; they gave their hard-earned money to a foundation for poor kids that paid Ronnie eighty percent of their donations. That's how he was able to afford the used ATVs and motorcycles, and Mike couldn't count the number of times his dad said: "don't you boys just love all the cool things I can buy for you?"

Jan wipes her hands on her apron and exhales before she turns to face her son. There is so much he doesn't know about his dad, so much Jan hid from her boys. From the bruises on her arms and legs to the words that hurt worse than any push, pinch, or grab.

"Last I heard, he was building a house outside of Harriman so he could be closer to the new dealership. His fourth wife should be happy there," Jan smirks and rolled her eyes. "I will never regret the children your father gave me, but I know now that I got out just before it got worse. There are a lot of things that you don't know, don't need to know."

"We witnessed how mean dad was, abusive. I know he had affairs, hell, most of the town knew. Sam and I weren't so young, but it still must have been really hard for you to hide your anger. I only remember you showing Sam and me how good our life was without Dad. Quiet. Peaceful. Fun. I hope you know that we appreciated that.

"We had the best life, Mom. I'm not sure what happened with Sam; he's made some really poor choices and I just pray that it's not too late for him to turn it around."

Chapter 5
DECEMBER 27, 2014

S un shines through the bare Oak tree branches into Mike's eyes as he turns into the Jones' U-shaped driveway. Although necessary, talking with Danny's parents about why their son decided to commit suicide and how it has affected those that loved him most will be the hardest thing Mike has ever done. He has been dreading this meeting for the past year. It can't wait any longer.

Danny's parents, Linda and Daniel Jones, Sr. moved from the modest home where Danny was raised in Oakdale to a spacious split-level brick home that overlooks Emory Golf Course in Harriman. Their living space doubled in size and tripled in value after Danny moved out, and so Linda and Daniel sold the place they raised their son.

It wasn't the easiest decision, but Harriman also offers more activities for an older couple than

Oakdale; the grocery store, shopping, and entertainment are just around the corner.

Mike shifts his mother's Buick into park and turns off the engine. He's not sure what to expect from Danny's parents; he hasn't seen them since he moved to California. Mrs. Jones sounded excited to get his call and eager to see him in person. Three deep breaths later, Mike lifts the flowers from the passenger seat and exits the car.

Linda answers the door within seconds of Mike ringing the bell. He doesn't have time to think before thin arms wrap around his neck and the scent of Chanel No. 5 reaches his nose. Daniel's baritone voice in the background reverberates. "Linda, let the poor boy inside. It's freezing out there."

Red lipstick from Linda's greeting smudges Mike's cheek and she wipes it with a wet thumb just like she used to when he and Danny were kids. As she backs away, tears pool in her bright eyes and she blinks them away.

"Mike. Oh, my gosh. I can hardly believe you're here. You look great, just as handsome as ever." Heat rises to Mike's face and he blushes at the compliment. "Let me put these beautiful roses in water before they wilt. Come in, sit down. Daniel and I are so thrilled that you're here."

Danny, your mom hasn't changed a bit. Still as little and lovely as ever. She was always my favorite. And your dad...Dude, you got so lucky. I hope you're watching so you can see how much you're missed and how loved you still are.

"MRS. JONES, lunch was fantastic. I don't remember the last time I had egg salad sandwiches and Ruffles. The wavy chips were always Danny's favorite. I can almost see him tossing his paper plate into the trash before pushing out the back screen door with the football in hand. We spent hours tossing that thing back and forth in your backyard. Best Christmas present I ever got."

"That football kept you out of some trouble after you boys got a little older. Not all the trouble, but some." Daniel's gruff laugh brought a smile to Mike's lips. "The antics I pushed under the rug for you two...I could write a book. '*How to be a Police Captain and cover up your son's petty crimes*' would most certainly be a best-seller."

"I saw Coach Smalls when I got to town," Mike said. "He told me that he had a hand in keeping me and Danny out of jail. The two of you had secondary full-time jobs following up on our so-called adventures. We must have made your life hell.

"Remember the one time we did get arrested, though? You were on vacation so there was nothing you could do to get us out of spending the night in jail. That was one of the worst nights of my life. My dad never knew anything about the trouble we made for you." Mike smiles as he shakes his head. Memories flood back and he misses his old friend.

His thoughts were interrupted by a sharp laugh from Daniel. "You honestly believe I couldn't do anything to free you two hoodlums because I was on vacation? Oh, now that's comical, probably the funniest thing I've heard all year. Son, I could have made one phone call and had y'all free in a minute. I chose not to; seems that holding you accountable for your actions was the right choice.

"And don't kid yourself, Mikey. Your dad knew. He just chose to handle it differently than I did." A wink from Daniel confirms that he and his own father had a completely opposite approach to parenting.

As they continue to catch up, Mike's eyes gaze in the direction of the bay window at the far side of the house, the past flashes in his mind. Instead of taking in the view of a large yard with a fire pit and old oaks at the edge of a golf green, Mike sees an image of his best friend.

Danny walks ahead of him on the trail that leads to the waterfall; their favorite spot to hang, think, and drink. It's the summer between Junior and Senior year. Each of them carries a brown paper bag in their hands and has a backpack slung over their shoulder. The east side of the Falls is the best place to sit which means they must cross the river.

From past experiences, the boys learned what they

needed to pack to enhance their time at the Falls. The backpacks held an array of supplies. Wet Shoes: once while crossing, Danny cut his foot on a sharp rock, so they both bought specific shoes to wear in the river. Towels: who knew when someone would get froggy and jump in. A Blanket: for when a girl showed up.

They change out of their hiking boots and into their wet shoes, cross the river, pull out towels to use as pads on the rocks, and crack a bottle of something that burns when it goes down. During this excursion, two girls show up and make themselves at home, not that Danny or Mike mind.

The girls drink the liquor that the boys brought and sit close to them on the towels that cover the rocks. Thankful that they were smart enough to bring a blanket, Danny and girl number one make their way down a trail for some privacy.

"I'M REALLY sorry I haven't been back to see y'all in so long. The two of you were like a second set of parents. It's just...well. Gosh, I don't even have a good excuse. I've just been selfish, I guess."

"Sweetheart, you don't need to apologize. You're here now. That's what matters." A genuine smile radiates from Linda's face like the sun is positioned behind her head. "Tell us the full story of how you got to L.A. We only know snippets."

"You remember when I Managed Red's?" Mike began. "Well, one night in 2004, close to Halloween, a man named Gene sat at the bar and told me what I thought was his life story. He traveled across the US for business, was never married, no kids, no pets; just worked.

"He was born in Virginia and always loved passing through East Tennessee. Small towns set in the mountains were his favorite places to visit; he said the best food was cooked in small-town bars.

"He worked for a transportation company as an Account Manager, so he visited his customers a few times a year. The first time he came in, we hit it off like we were old friends. By the time he passed away, I would have called him family.

"Every year, he brought me a Christmas gift and he made it a point to come to Oakdale in the late spring when the rivers ran fastest and the waterfalls were strong. He and I would meet up with Lisa, Amanda, and Danny and have drinks out at Falls. He actually told me one drunken night that he thought I hung the moon. It wasn't even weird when he said it."

Mike smiles to himself at the memory of his friend expressing his feelings. Linda is so enthralled with the story that she rarely blinks. Daniel nods his head and smiles as if he's listening to his favorite author read from a novel.

"I didn't hear from him for about six months and I thought maybe he got a new job or something. I never would have believed that he was in a car accident.

"From what I read in the papers, he was driving his Porsche down Highway 1, south of Los Angeles, and a drunk driver crossed the center line, hitting Gene head-on. The car burst into flames; he never had a chance. God rest his soul." Tears well in Mike's eyes and he wipes them away, apologizing.

"His lawyer contacted me the next week and what do you know, I became an instant millionaire at 28 years old. Based on how Gene carried himself, I would have never pegged him for a pretentious, snooty, rich dude. He was so down-to-Earth, so chill.

"He left me everything he owned. Imagine my surprise. I now live in a 19,000-square-foot home that overlooks the Pacific Ocean, I have a private jet, four luxury cars, including a freaking Lamborghini, and all the money I could ever imagine. It's surreal; still today, I can hardly believe it.

"First thing I did was buy my mom that house. She loves it and I'm so happy for her. My dad got the dealership, and my brother is homeless. How does that make sense? But that's a different story for a different day." Mike shakes his head.

Daniel leans forward and places his elbows on his knees. "So, how did a traveling salesman make millions? Sounds like I chose the wrong career."

"I guess that does sound pretty strange, doesn't

it? He only worked so he could travel and keep his mind fresh. He enjoyed what he did and he was a natural people person. The millions came from his tenure with the Detroit Lions; he was their kicker for seven years."

"Gene? Kicker for the Lions?" Daniel's eyes squint as he racks his brain to remember the old Detroit NFL team's players. "Oh, my goodness. You mean Eugene "Uey" La Port?"

"The one and only. He made some very smart money choices and, voila, millions. So, I picked up and moved to L.A., partied my ass off for a year, threw my money around, and met a girl.

"Rebecca is a model; she fits the mold for a millionaire's wife. We have the same friends at the same parties and like to spend money on everything and nothing. So, we got married. But..." Mike purses his lips and takes a deep breath as he thinks how to politely describe his marriage.

"Honestly, material things just aren't doing it for me, anymore. I came home because my mom asked for help with Stevie, but when I'm not lying to myself, I'm here to find me. To come back to the person I am, truly. To be the son, brother, and best friend that God wants me to be."

"IT'S BEEN A YEAR, but I don't think it will ever get easier to talk about what happened. About why our son decided to take his own life. I can't even begin to describe how much I miss him, my only child. I wouldn't wish this pain on anyone, even my fiercest enemy."

Linda does her darndest to hold back the tears but is unsuccessful. A moment later, she takes a deep breath and continues.

"You know the stages of grief; I went through them all not knowing what was happening to me. At first, I was in denial—'There is no way Danny committed suicide, the letter must have been a sick joke.' I called him for days, praying he would pick up the phone."

Tears roll down her cheeks and she dabs at them with a tissue. "Then I got mad. How could he do this to me and his father? Honestly, I'm still a little angry. The 'if only' stage came next. Blaming myself for not doing whatever it was I thought at the time I could have done to save him, didn't bring him back."

Mike recognizes the emotion and focuses on Linda's face. Everything around them fades away.

"For a while, I thought I might be going mad. Each time I looked in the mirror and tried to smile, my grin just faded. I couldn't even fake it. Again, and again, I prayed if there was a Lord above for Him to give me something to believe in. I thank God every day that Daniel talked me into going to a counselor who referred me to a psychiatrist.

"That very well may have saved my life. He put me on depression medication until I was able to get over the hump and finally accept that my son is gone."

Unable to contain her grief, Linda sobs into her hands and Mike waits for her to continue, but she shakes her head, unable to go on without becoming distraught.

Mike offers his own story. "I understand. I went through the same stages. Obviously, nothing near what you had to endure, though. One of my close friends, Saul, is a psychologist. He offered to hear my story but getting that deep with someone while mixing friendship wasn't something I wanted to do.

"I chose to talk with a local pastor, which helped a lot." Mike's voice cracks and he folds his hands in his lap. Tears begin to fall and he squeezes his eyes shut before gasping for a breath.

"You know, Mike, when Danny was ten, he told us that your Uncle Dominic had been inappropriate with him."

Daniel's voice startles Mike and his head snaps to attention at the sound of his uncle's name. "What? Uncle Dominic? I don't understand." Mike shakes his head in disbelief.

"We made sure that Danny didn't have a chance to be alone with Dominic after that day. Danny begged us not to tell anyone, said that he was just scared, but I felt compelled to tell your mother. If nothing else, to be sure she was aware of what had happened.

"It was inconceivable to think that the town Preacher might have been inappropriate with our son. The last thing we wanted was for something like this to happen to another young boy. Especially you, Mike.

"Without any proof, all we could really do was keep a close eye on all of the kids around the church and pray. We prayed every day that God would keep the children of Oakdale safe."

"We had no idea how long it continued until Danny mailed this letter from California the day he died," Linda adds and offers the folded, white-lined notebook paper, worn from being handled often, to Mike.

He grasps the two-page letter from Linda's hand and begins to read.

DECEMBER 24, 2013

Dear Mom and Dad,

There is something that I have kept secret for over 20 years. Something that would shock the entire town of Oakdale if it ever came out. This is so hard to say, so I'm just going to say it.

Dominic McKay started touching me when I was just ten

years old. I don't even remember how it started. He made me promise to never tell a soul. By the time I was thirteen we had an understanding; he gave me gifts and money to do things that any normal teenage boy would never do. Especially with the town Preacher.

He told me that he loved me, he told me that God wanted us to be together, but I never felt right about what we did. I didn't like it, but I couldn't resist him. He was so smooth with his words, he talked me into staying every time I said I was going to leave.

I finally found the courage to break away after graduation. No one knew, not even my best friend. Mike would have killed his uncle if he knew; that's something I never doubted. Dominic called me Sam once, so I know that I wasn't the only one. I knew he had sinned with my best friend's brother and I never told. I made it a point to be the last boy he hurt.

Tryouts for the Braves were the day after I threatened to expose him for who he truly was. We had a huge argument that made me anxious and fail at the only thing I ever wanted to do. The only thing I truly loved.

When he found out that I choked at tryouts, he swore he would never do it again and started giving me more than just an allowance. He paid my rent, then my mortgage when I bought my first house, and my car payment, and most of my bills.

After he was finally arrested for embezzlement and other boys were safe, I cut all ties with him and found a shrink. I was finally starting to heal. I know it wasn't my fault and that he was wrong to use his position in the community to gain my trust.

Two months ago, when he found out he had Stage Four

Pancreatic Cancer, he sent me a reminder of the days he used me. A photo of me standing next to him at the cabin where he would take me to be alone. The place that I let him do things to me that I could never believe in my heart were the right things to do with a grown man.

I knew he would reveal that I was the 'friend' he kept and the entire world would believe his twisted explanation. Everyone would think that I blackmailed him into paying for everything. In a way, I am just as guilty as him; I accepted the money in exchange for silence.

How would it look to the fine upstanding citizens of Oakdale that the son of the police captain propositioned him, a preacher, to the point of harassment? If anyone believed his story, it would ruin my life. Who would believe a punk-ass kid over a small-town preacher man?

I barely spent any of the money Dominic gave me; I only bought the necessities of life. I felt awful about letting him have that kind of control over me. Money can only buy so much, though. Obviously, happiness is the furthest emotion from my mind.

Heartbroken doesn't even come close to describing how I feel; I'm sure you will understand when you read this letter because you will be heartbroken, too. There is no way I could let you down when all of this came out. Mike would never understand, either. There is no other way to escape this prison that I put myself in.

I am so sorry. Please forgive me.

All my love for eternity,

Danny

.   .   .

HOT TEARS DRIP down Mike's cheeks, matching those of his best friend's mother. "Are you okay, Mike?"

Mike excuses himself to the bathroom, so he can be sick.

~

HOW COULD this person I call family be the sole reason for my best friend to leave this earth? Danny, what the fuck, dude? Why didn't you tell me?

Pacing from one end of the living room to the other, Mike tries to work it out in his mind. Daniel and Linda follow his stride as if watching a tennis match.

"I'm even more confused, now. I have so many questions. How could I have not known this happened when we spent every minute together as kids? Why wouldn't he say anything about Dominic? I always wondered how he had the sweetest cars when he worked the shittiest jobs. Oh, man. That makes so much sense.

"All the times we drank and told honest stories; you know the saying that liquor is truth serum? Well, that was certainly true on my end. I told him things I would never think to say out loud without liquid courage. How could he keep this from me?

"I'm just so angry. Why would he take the easy

way out and leave everyone else with a mess to clean up? That's the most selfish thing I have ever heard of. My best friend would never do that to me." His voice softens and he says, "I miss him so much."

Mike slumps in a designer chair and lowers his head into his hands as he realizes that it's sadness that fuels the anger. Palms wipe away tears that stream down his face. He doesn't realize that he is the one repeating, "I'm sorry, Danny. I'm so sorry," until Linda kneels next to his chair and puts a warm hand on his knee. "How can I help you, son?"

Mike wraps her in an emotional hug and weeps.

ORANGE, red, and fuchsia streaks paint the whisps of clouds over Oakdale as the sun sets. Even though it was out of the way to his mom's house, Mike is drawn here to process the discussions of the day. He used to drive Lisa to this lookout while they were in high school. Even then, he appreciated the beauty of God's paintbrush.

Leaves blow in the same wind that moves Mike's hair off his forehead. Hot tears pool in his eyes and Mike blames the cool air at first. The Buick's stereo is tuned to XM's Hair Nation and turned up loud enough to be heard through the foliage as Mike finds his favorite rock.

Trees surround the natural Granite bench; one

stands out above the rest. Mike and Lisa carved their initials under a heart filled with AM + AS. Each time they found themselves tangled in each other's arms the lovebirds wondered who else fell in love at this overlook.

Thoughts of Danny and their life together drown out any memories of Lisa. Mr. and Mrs. Jones knew that Danny was at least touched by Uncle Dominic but felt that they couldn't press charges without more proof.

What would have changed if they pressed charges? God. Do I really have to go through all the stages of grief, again? Okay. I've denied it, been angry, and now it's the 'what if' stage. Let's see if I can get through all this in one day. Next up is depression.

Dude, that was rough. I hate seeing your mom cry. She loves you so much. And I can see that your dad blames himself. I blame me, too. Even though I know there is nothing I could do, I wish I would have had the chance to beat the shit out of my uncle for making your life a living hell.

Mike tries again and again to stop the tears that stream down his face as snapshots of better days fill the space behind his eyelids. He is unsuccessful until "Something to Believe In" by Poison plays through the speakers.

Sometimes I wish to God
I didn't know now
The things I didn't know then

It feels like Danny is there with Mike for a

moment. *How about this song, Danny? Your favorite. If this record wasn't released in 1990 when we were only eight years old, I would swear someone wrote this song about our life today. Are you sure you didn't sell the lyrics to Poison in some sick premonition? That would be just like you, you know.*

The conversation with Danny is interrupted by the vibration of Mike's cell phone.

Rebecca's name lights up the screen.

You always did know how to ruin a good thing.

A ding signals a voicemail. Without listening to it, Mike types out a text.

Mike: *Be home next Sunday. I need some time to grieve for my best friend. I met with Danny's parents today.*

Rebecca: *Let it go, Mike. Come home. I won't wait forever for you.*

Dumbfounded at the blatant selfishness of the woman he married; Mike instantly gets over any attraction he felt for his soon-to-be ex-wife. He wonders to himself how he could have fallen for such a shallow person.

Road, you gotta take me home.

Chapter 6
DECEMBER 28, 2014

"**E**xcuse me, miss. How can I donate directly to CATS? All of the silent auction items are fantastic, but I just want to give some money as my way to support the kitties." Red and white dominate the Santa hat Christmas sweater the grey-haired lady wears, her checkbook and pen in hand.

"Miss Ellen, the CATS fundraiser was last month. Today we are here to support the Jefferson Middle School choir; they need new robes and songbooks. If you would like to donate to them, Mary Lou will gladly accept your check at the table across the room." Lisa Johnson dons her most sincere smile and puts her arm around the elderly lady as she leads her toward the cashier.

"Oh, that's right. Thank you, dear."

"MOM, did you bring me to this fundraiser for any specific reason?" Mike is unable to take his eyes from the tall brunette across the room helping an old lady figure out how to donate; her smile is captivating.

"But of course, dear. You're rich; you should donate some money to your nephew's school." Jan smiles, satisfied with her match-making skills.

"I could just as easily write a check," Mike's gaze is fixed on the Seventh Grade Geography teacher.

"Yes, dear, but then I wouldn't have the satisfaction of this moment. The way you look at Lisa has not changed. Go." Jan nudges her son.

Mike is unable to stop his feet from taking him directly to his one and only true love. After moving to L.A., Mike tried to find someone he could love as much as Lisa but when he met Rebecca and decided to marry, he gave up on that dream. He told himself that it was less messy, less painful, to become an actor and let everyone think he and Rebecca were in love.

Lisa had been through successes and failures with Mike, during their relationship, and continued to love him for the person that he was. She did her best to help guide him through the hard times until he pushed her away and gave up on their relationship. Something he regrets every day.

God, she's gorgeous. She hasn't changed a bit. Danny, you catching this, dude?

As he approaches from behind, Mike covers Lisa's eyes with his hands, and she flinches.

The scent of a cologne Lisa has only smelled on one man in her life reaches her nose.

Creed? That can't be Louis; he has much smaller hands.

After she and Mike broke up, Lisa dated a man that wined and dined her for a year before she broke his heart. He was a self-made millionaire and spent more money than Lisa could imagine ever having. This cologne, Creed, was his favorite.

Mike stands close and whispers low in his high school sweetheart's ear. "Guess who, Lisa?"

After releasing an unintentional gasp, she replies, "Mikey? I would know the way you say my name anywhere!" She turns to find the man who made her heart race all through high school standing so close she could smell minty mouthwash.

As she raises her eyes to meet his, she becomes dizzy. Mike's hands fall to her waist, keeping her close; smiles instinctive on both of their lips,

"God, you look great! Oh, I'm sorry. You're probably married." A frown tugs her lips down and she apologizes for being too forward. "Is your wife with you?" Pink touches Lisa's cheeks and she turns her head from side to side searching for an angry woman.

"No," Mike responds as his hands drop to his side.

Lisa's smile widens.

"She's not here," he adds with pursed lips.

Lisa takes a step back and peers around Mike's

shoulder at Jan, who clears her throat. "Miss Johnson, it's so nice to see you. How is the fundraiser going?"

"Great, Mrs. Higgenbottom. Thanks so much for coming. Did you peruse all the awesome silent auction items? I think there is a vacation package for somewhere warm and sandy up for bid." Not missing a beat, the seasoned volunteer is familiar with her regular supporters.

MIKE PUTS his phone back in his pocket and asks his mom if she's okay going home by herself. "Of course, Mike. Who was on the phone?" Red lipstick slides back into the tube before it drops into Jan's purse.

"Coach Smalls has agreed to pick me up; I'm hoping Lisa will join me for a ride around town. I can't stop all the questions popping in my head; I must have more time with her."

"Oh, yes. By all means. I just love that girl." With a smirk, Jan adds "I won't wait up." Mike is not able to contain a throaty laugh.

On the stage, volunteers total the amount of donations as they smile and laugh. An older lady with red hair piled high in a bun adds up checks while two other volunteers count the cash. An audible gasp accompanies an "oh, my" as the red-haired lady places her hand over her heart and scans one check for a second and third time. Showing the check to other volunteers, she mouths "ten-thousand dollars?".

You're welcome. The one thing Mike promised himself, after it sunk in that he was a millionaire, is that he would give to grass-roots organizations as often as he had the opportunity.

Lisa steps up to the microphone and asks for everyone's attention. "Tonight's silent auction has raised more than $20,000 for the Jefferson Middle School Choir." Applause causes Lisa to pause the announcement. "Thank you to everyone who bid on auction items; I hope you thoroughly enjoy your purchase.

"To those of you who donated money, thank you so very much for your support. All of the teachers at Jefferson appreciate the fantastic community in which we live. Enjoy the rest of your night."

Mike raises his chin in Lisa's direction and she starts toward him. After shaking hands with guests and thanking donors, she finally makes it across the room.

"Hi there," pink returns to her cheeks and she wonders why she has such a hard time catching her breath. "I bet your mom can't wait to book that trip to Cancun."

"Yeah, she can't stop talking about it. Hey, do you have plans for the rest of the night? I would love to catch up." Eyebrows raise in hopes of spending more time with Lisa.

"Oh," Lisa frowns and Mike's face mirrors hers. "Um, Mike. You told me that you're married."

"Look, I'm not asking you to board a plane to Paris," tilting his head, Mike adds, "but that's not a bad idea."

Lisa rolls her eyes widening her smile.

"That's my girl. I just want to talk with an old friend. Let's get out of here." Mike reaches for Lisa's hand with a familiar twinkle in his eye.

COACH SMALLS HOLDS the door open for Lisa as she climbs into the backseat of a black Lincoln limousine. Mike winks at his driver, teacher, friend before ducking his head and closing the door.

"I heard Coach Smalls started a driving company but have never had a reason to hire him. This is great, Mike. I love that you are investing in the community where your mother and nephew live. Speaking of, I heard there was a very large check in tonight's donation, that wasn't from you, was it?"

In her own way, Lisa hoped it was from him, proving that he didn't lose his good heart when he inherited millions. But at the same time, she hoped he was not the doner so she would be able to ward off these emotions.

Fantasies of what she would say and how she

would act if Mike ever came back to Oakdale stopped popping up a year or so after he left. Honestly, she didn't expect to see Mike again. Ever.

The fact that she forgot every word she had rehearsed over and over again didn't really surprise her. Lisa never stopped loving Mike, even when she dated other people. What did surprise her, is how she felt like a schoolgirl when he looked at her. She could feel herself blush and hoped he couldn't tell.

"I hope it was enough. My mom told me the amount of your final goal and I wasn't sure how much was already donated, so figured half would be okay."

"Yes, Mike. It was very generous. Thank you."

"You're welcome. It's the least I could do for my nephew's school. My mom has also filled me in on what Stevie has been going through and I really want to sit with you and discuss his behavior, but not tonight. Is that okay? Am I being selfish by leaving the subject of my nephew for another time?" Mike's gaze warms Lisa's insides. She hasn't experienced this feeling since Mike left for L.A.

Lisa dated a few men over the past five years; in her eyes, no one was as funny or smart as Mike. Or sexy. No other man could recreate the heat she and Mike shared. It was as if every time they touched, a shock literally passed through Lisa's body. When talking with her girlfriends, she compared their intimacy to fireworks.

"I understand. I would love to discuss Stevie and how Jan has been involved, but my heart isn't there tonight, either. You're not being selfish. We can arrange to chat another time."

The limo slows to a halt in front of the entrance of AK Bissell Park. A line of cars putts along the one-way road, passing Christmas light displays in different colors and scenes. The windows roll down and *"O Holy Night"* fills the car along with cool Tennessee air.

Gotta love Smalls. He's one romantic dude.

"Oak Ridge leaves these lights up for the entire month of December. I haven't had a chance to drive through yet this year. I want every one of these displays in my front yard. Ooh, grazing reindeer. This is my favorite so far."

Lisa fails at the attempt to hide her excitement. Bright brown eyes twinkle with the flashing lights timed to Christmas music. "This is so nice, Mike. Thank you for bringing me here tonight."

Lisa's face lights up as she gazes at the holiday displays. Mike's expression mirrors hers as he watches Lisa, his first love. The happiness they share in that moment transports him to a better time—a simpler time—when he and Lisa were planning their life together.

She used to smile just like this at all of Mike's antics until he pushed it too far. It was way too easy to become a drunk while managing Red's. He will never forgive himself for treating Lisa like she didn't matter to him. Mike would give anything to change the last days of their relationship. A heaviness pulls his shoulders forward and forces him to look out the window, away from Lisa.

"I lost track of you, Mike." A whisper brings him back to reality and he turns toward her voice. Lisa's head is bent to observe her red nails that play with a button on her coat. "I followed your every move until one day you were gone. Poof, just like that." She lifts her eyes to gaze into Mike's, stealing his breath. "How does that happen?"

"Allen," Mike manages to utter.

"Who is Allen?"

"Me, Lisa. I changed my last name from Higgenbottom to Allen."

"What? That's ridiculous. You can't just change your last name. Can you?"

Mike nods.

"So, all those times I wrote Lisa Higgenbottom on my folders, I could have been writing Lisa Allen? It just doesn't seem the same." Her giggles at that moment remind Mike of high school weekends spent in Danny's basement with their girlfriends, trying not to wake the parents.

Coach Smalls opens Lisa's door and offers his hand as she exits. Mike follows her out of the vehicle and places his hand on the small of her back. Colorful lights flash around them as they make their way to the center of the park. Captivated with each other, they don't notice the dozens of vehicles that pass them.

"You followed my every move? Really?" In his mind, Mike replays the last time he laid eyes on Lisa before leaving for L.A. They had broken up a few weeks prior to Mike receiving his inheritance and she refused to meet with him to talk about making it work. In her mind, they had already said everything there was to say.

The day he flew to L.A., he drove past her house and saw her in the arms of another man. A short shake of his head pushes the unhappy thought to the side.

From the corner of her eye, she sees his frown and understands his mindset. "Let's sit," Lisa positions her coat under her backside as she lowers herself to the cold cement bench near the fountain. "Tell me every-thing that you've been up to over the past five years."

"We may freeze to death if I do that," Mike winks sending chills down Lisa's spine from more than the cold. "I have a lot of great stories to share with you, but I want to share the best one first. See, in Califor-nia, people throw a lot of extremely expensive dinner parties for their friends to gather and get sloshed, all disguised as a fundraiser.

"The best fundraiser I have ever attended, though, hands down, was around Christmastime at a local school that needed to find a way to pay for the student's choir costumes or something. I was told it was a reason to donate some money to help the community, so I agreed to go."

"Are you talking about a local California school?" Lisa raises her eyebrows; she remembers how her Mike would tell stories about outrageous adventures they were on and make it sound like something they weren't currently doing.

"No, Lisa, I'm not." Turning to face her, Mike reaches for her hand and follows his motion with his eyes. Lisa instinctively grasps onto Mike like he never left. "I can't believe how much I have missed this town. My family." Mike raises his eyes from their hands to meet the same big brown eyes that made his mouth dry and his thoughts scatter. "You."

When he looks at Lisa, he can't remember why he left Tennessee. Just like old times, her smile melts away any anxiety he harbors.

"Mike?"

He hadn't noticed that his face was so close to Lisa's; another inch and his lips would touch hers. Clearing his throat, he remembers that he is still married and forces distance between them, releasing her hand. "I'm sorry, Lisa. I must be caught up in the season. Where are my manners?"

A warm smile spreads across her lips, reaching her eyes, and she takes a deep breath before standing. "Ready?"

∾

"REMEMBER the first time we snuck you and Amanda into Danny's basement?" Coach turns on Dale Rd. and stops in front of the house on the corner. "I thought for sure your loud-ass giggles would wake his parents. Man, that was a great night."

"We were so nervous. I mean, we were sixteen sneaking into Captain Jones' house. What were we thinking?" Lisa leans forward to get a better look out the window. "We had our first kiss, here, Mike."

"I had to do something to keep you quiet," Mike smirks.

As Lisa turns toward Mike, she starts to reach for him as she did that night but lowers her hand before he notices, reminding herself that he is married and she is not interested in rekindling an old flame; she leans back into the leather seat.

As much as she still feels a strong connection, a spark, Lisa is unsure if Mike is still a heavy drinker and how much he has changed, if at all. It hurts too much to lose the one person who sincerely completes her; she knows from experience.

The old house is dark, so Mike and Lisa get out to stretch their legs knowing that they will not disturb anyone. Coach turns off the engine, anticipating they could be a while. With their backs leaning against the Lincoln, each trapped in their individual memories, words escape them for some time.

"How many beers did we take from the fridge in the basement? God, it must have been at least a six-pack every Friday and Saturday night. I have no idea how they were replenished without question. You girls would follow us anywhere, wouldn't you? The Falls were just the best."

"Oh, my gosh. The Falls. Mikey," Lisa's smirk turns to a wide smile in seconds, then fades to a frown. "I haven't thought about that place since we..."

"Yeah. I know. We used to take Gene there every time he came into town. Remember? He had a blast with the younger crowd. We sure knew how to have fun in this little town. The big city sure is a different world. I was talking to Danny the other day and..."

"What?" Lisa interrupts. "You were talking to Danny?"

"I was," Mike exhales before he faces Lisa. "It's my way of holding on, I guess. I talk to Danny. A lot. Is that weird? Never mind, I know it is."

"No, Mike. It's not weird." Lisa reaches for Mike and places her hand on his cheek. Two-day scruff tickles her palm like it had when they spent summer nights in Danny's basement after graduation. The temptation to kiss Mike overpowers Lisa and she places her lips on his.

Turning to face her, Mike wraps one arm around Lisa's waist and stares into her eyes long enough for the flame to reignite. His fingers position her chin so his lips mesh with hers for a short but significant display of affection. For Lisa, the kiss represents the past melting into their future.

"I've missed you so much, Mike." Lisa's breath in his ear causes his arms to pull her closer.

After the embrace that brings them back to reality, tears threatened to spill and Mike blinks then away before he turns to gaze at his best friend's empty house. "I can't believe he's gone. It's just not fair. I had lunch with Danny's parents yesterday and learned some disturbing details of his life. I should have seen that he was depressed and troubled. I missed it."

Mike lowers his head, allowing his hair to fall in his face before regaining control. Searching Lisa's eyes for understanding, he continues, "I want to share so much with you, but I hope you can understand that now, here, isn't the right time. I just miss him so much, Lisa. I never got to say goodbye. I would give anything to hear his voice again."

THE LINCOLN IS LEFT RUNNING in front of Lisa's brick ranch on Culver Rd. as Mike and Lisa continue their conversation.

"Living so close to work must have its advantages," Mike observes the small home before flashing a smile to Lisa. "This neighborhood seems nice and quiet. Your house must be very cozy."

"After I landed the teaching position, I purchased

this place. It's just the right size for a single teacher; a starter home is what the Realtor called it. My neighbors are fantastic. We all watch out for each other and are around if anyone needs help. The half-mile is perfect walking distance. I sure do save money on wear and tear on my car, not to mention fuel."

She was aware she was rambling, but they were at a precipice and Lisa didn't want to be the one to fall in. Mike was back, but she had no clue for how long. "Look, Mike. I would love to invite you in, but..."

"No, it's okay. I have really enjoyed our time together. Thank you for agreeing to join me and reminisce. I have missed you more than I realized; it would be a lie if I said my heart didn't leap when I saw you, tonight."

"Being back here is surreal, to say the least; so much has happened over the years. I certainly have been gone for too long. My main focus is Stevie and I need to make sure I do everything I can to help him."

"Listen, let's find some time to discuss Stevie later this week." Deep in Lisa's purse is a business card with her contact information.

The principal of Jefferson Middle School has the philosophy that parents need to have a relationship with their children's teachers, therefore supplies business cards for the staff. She hands one to Mike, kisses his cheek, and places her hand on the door handle. "Thank you for tonight. Call me."

Coach opens Lisa's door and offers his hand once again.

～

TINT on the Lincoln's window dulls the view of homeless people sleeping on a cold, dark street like bodies in an open grave. Mike's thoughts instantly turn to his brother.

Is Sam warm? When was the last time he ate? Is he cele-brating Christmas alone? Does he miss Stevie? Is he drugged-up? In a shelter?

As they pass underneath a broken old billboard that used to read "Jesus saves," Mike swears Sam comes into view standing next to a fire contained in a burn barrel.

For a split-second, Mike considers asking Coach to slow down but stops himself before he has to explain to his friend why he would want to put himself in danger. This area of town is known to not be safe; un-fortunately, it is the most direct path home.

What would I even say at this point? 'Hey, bro. What's up?' That doesn't even make sense. How could I be so noncha-lant? It's been so long and so much has happened.

Sam's worst decisions were made after I left; I wasn't here to help him. Would I have been able to compete with drugs? Would it have made things worse? What am I think-ing…how could it be any worse? Stupid question, eh, Danny?

What if I did come face to face with Sam? Would he even

remember me? How bad is his mind, really? Would he resent me for leaving him here?

I pray that it wasn't a mistake coming home. Why am I thinking about how this affects me? This is all about Stevie; I need to change how I view this entire situation. I need to help my nephew no matter how hard it is on me. He needs me.

"I swear I saw Sam last night." Mike slices potatoes with an ulu that Jan picked up on a trip to Alaska as his mother mixes the meat for today's lunch. It's been ages since Mike has prepared any food; the chef is paid well.

His stomach growls in anticipation of his mom's latest experimental dish, Meatloaf. Sausage is added to the traditional ground beef for a zestier flavor and barbecue sauce replaces ketchup as the topping.

"If you were anywhere near the Home Depot, I'm sure you did. From what I hear, they have a fire every night and can be heard singing all the way to the Middle School."

Jan turns toward her son, tilts her head, and continues. "You know, when I think about it, Sam is kind of like Bigfoot — there are sightings of him all the time, but no one really knows if he exists."

"I'm not sure if I'm supposed to laugh or not, but honestly, Mom, that was pretty funny." Mike attempts to squash the smirk that forms on his lips.

Shooing away the negativity with a wave of a sticky hand, Jan explains. "I've gotten used to the fact that my oldest son is homeless while I live in a house that is far too large for Stevie and me. I used to worry about cold weather, days like this past week, but there are places he can go if he needs to.

"Your brother has put himself into an extremely sad situation, but the life he lives is his choice. If he ever wants to change his ways, he knows where to find me.

"I have given way too much of my happiness away on dreams for Sam. At this point in my life, I enjoy what I can and don't stress about what I am unable to control." Jan turns toward her son and continues, "It has taken three years of counseling just to say that phrase without crying."

"How does Stevie feel about his dad living so close to where he attends school? Lisa told me she over-heard one student teasing him because his dad is homeless. Is that part of the reason he has been giving you problems?"

Mike feels the need to gauge Stevie's mindset so when he meets with Lisa, he can prepare to discuss the best way to handle the trouble he has had with other kids at school. Jan tells him that Stevie has been in three fights this year alone.

"In September, after the second fight, is when I called asking you to come home."

"Three? Wow, that's pretty good for a thirteen-year-old kid."

"It's not good, Michael," Jan scowls and scoops the meat mixture into a baking dish.

"That's not what I meant, Mom. I meant for such a young guy, getting into three fights is a lot. What started them, do you know? Has he talked to you about any of this?" A scowl forms on Mike's face, pulling his eyebrows into a 'V'. Setting down the knife, he focuses on Jan's words.

"He hasn't said much to me directly, just that it sucks to be different. All of his friends at least have either a mom or a dad, but no one lives with their grandmother. When I was young, I was different, too, so I understand some of his pain.

"My parents were divorced, which was pretty uncommon in the '60s. Just like Stevie and Sam, your uncle Dominic was in a few fights in his day, too. Your Grandpa had his problems with alcohol and other substances, so our home life wasn't much better than what you had to put up with before I left your dad."

"Mom, you did your best."

"I know, Mike. I can never make it up to you boys, but I will never stop apologizing for what you had to endure." With a final nod, Jan turns to the sink to wash her hands

Not the right time to bring up Dominic. I need to ask some tough questions, but when the time is right.

"Well, did he at least win? Was he the instigator or was he getting picked on?" Details of the aggression, or lack thereof, will assist Mike with how to approach Stevie.

If he started the fights, he could be a bully and needs to know that's not the way to be a man. On the other hand, if he was defending himself, he should be rewarded in some way, but taught how to communicate first. Poor kid has been through too much sorrow in his young life.

"He had a black eye and bloody nose after the first fight, a black eye and bloody knuckles after the second, and bloody knuckles this last time. I would say he's progressively improving," Jan frowns with one side of her mouth.

"Sounds a lot like his dad's middle school days. I'm just worried that he might fall into the same sort of crowd. It's all I can do to stay upbeat and let him know I'm here. One day he will be too old to open up to his old Grandma and I'm afraid that day is racing towards us."

One arm wraps around Jan's shoulders as her son pulls her close for a warm embrace. Mike knows he needs to make up for lost time. "I'm so sorry I didn't come home sooner, Mom."

VOICES BOUNCE off the walls and reach teenage ears at the top of the stairs. Fingers ball into fists as Stevie overhears the conversation between his Uncle Mike and his grandma. Anger heats him from the inside out; he doesn't care what anyone says, he's not anything like his dad. After listening for a few minutes, he starts down the stairs with loud steps.

"Are you just now getting up?" Mike glances at his Rolex; "It's almost 11 o'clock."

Stevie walks past Mike without looking at him and turns his back to open the fridge.

"Stevie?" Silence.

"Hey, Bud. Aren't you going to answer me?"

Milk jostles inside the clear jug as Stevie sets it on the counter with a thud. Glaring at Mike, he opens the container and pours a full glass without taking his eyes off his uncle.

"Wow. What's all that about?"

With shaggy hair hanging in his face, Stevie squints and remains silent as he returns the milk to the refrigerator.

"Hey, I'm just trying to say hi, Stevie. Please don't be rude."

Sneakers squeak on the granite floor as Stevie turns to address his uncle. "You think I'm a pussy, that I can't take care of myself. You think that because my dad is a fucking loser, I'm going to end up a loser, too."

"Well, for starters, that language in front of your

grandmother is unacceptable. Please don't do that again. Secondly, I never said you couldn't take care of yourself or that you would end up a loser. Honestly, I think quite the opposite. I think that if you have some help you will accomplish great things."

"What do you care what happens in my life?" Stevie interrupts his uncle. "You haven't bothered to come see me in, like, five years. Now all of a sudden you wanna play like you care? You think you can just jump back into my life and boss me around? That's bullshit, dude. Go play your big shot routine on someone who gives a fuck."

Letting the language slide, Mike understands that his nephew needs more than a lecture. "Stevie, look..."

"Don't call me that. I'm not a kid. It's Steve. My name is Steve."

"You're right, you are not a kid anymore. I apologize. You've grown so much since I last saw you, Steve."

"Whatever," accompanies an eye-roll.

As Steve turns away, Mike reaches out for him, one hand grips his shoulder to turn his nephew to face him. A loud crack sounds in Mike's ears before the ache reaches his senses, his jaw pulses in rhythm with his heartbeat.

Steve stands in front of him with balled fists and black pupils. Heavy pants cause his shoulders to rise and fall with a dramatic flair.

"Michael!" Jan's shriek is as distant as the neighbor's barking dog.

Without missing a beat, Mike pulls Steve into a bear hug before he can escape. Steve wails his arms inside the tight embrace, but Mike holds him tight. With his arms trapped against his sides, Steve gives in to his anger and his entire body starts to shake, sobs escape his throat. Relaxing his grip to release the pressure, but still holding firm, Mike turns the embrace into a hug.

Steve grips his uncle around his waist, hanging on for dear life as Mike spies his mom across the room. Jan stands still with her hand over her mouth as she waits for her son to say something. He nods at his mother as hope fills his eyes.

"It's okay, bud. I'm here to help."

FLAMES dance in the stone fireplace, Mike's face grows warm from the heat. He stands near the living room mantle and closes his eyes. Lisa's image appears in his mind, making Mike smile.

The scent of pumpkin pie fills the family room as Jan turns on the candle warmer before she sits on the loveseat in front of the bay window. Not expecting anyone to join him, Mike flinches.

"I'm sorry, Mike. Did I startle you?"

With a hearty chuckle, Mike shakes his head. "Just thinking is all."

"A penny for your thoughts," Jan replies before the coffee mug reaches her lips. Another mug filled with steaming liquid sits on the coffee table.

Mike smiles to himself. *Cheapskate.* "Just a penny?" he teases, then grows more serious. Soft cushions sink under Mike as he lowers himself to the couch with the mug in his hand. "You know when I left it was kind of like the perfect storm in my life. Red's was losing money, so I was probably going to lose my job; I was drinking way too much; Lisa broke up with me; my brother didn't want to hang out with me anymore.

"I figured *'what the hell, I might as well go live my dream in California. After all, I have a house there, I should at least visit, right?'* I know y'all warned me that it might be too much too fast, but I was hellbent on getting out of here.

"What was the phrase you used? *Don't get too big for your britches.* I never knew how much I missed the South until I got back. The way I saw it, L.A. was a chance to be a better person — different. Boy was that a life lesson."

Mike takes a sip from the mug Jan hands him. Hot coffee laced with Bailey's Irish Cream warms him from the inside out. His sigh of pleasure makes Jan grin. There's a reason it's her favorite drink.

"I bet it was, dear. You've enjoyed your time in California, though, and have had such great opportunities. Your friend must have thought the world of you to leave you his entire estate. The gorgeous house with an ocean view, the cars, the lifestyle.

"You have met some incredible people and were able to become a successful man instead of just someone who has money. I am so proud of the selfless man that is my son; your donations to those who are in need makes my heart swell.

"Building houses for injured soldiers remains my favorite charity that you give to. Coming in a close second, though, has to be funding college grants in Gene's name for twenty low-income kids every year. Just when I think I can't love you more, you share another experience with me that proves me wrong."

In his pocket, Mike's phone vibrates. He has already changed the contact information from *Wife* to *Bec*, which makes him smirk; she hates that nickname. Sliding the red 'End' icon, he ignores Rebecca's call for the third time in twelve hours.

Without missing a beat, Mike responds to Jan, "Giving makes me happy, Mom, I'm so thankful that Gene left me the means to do what I can. It's been a great ride and I've had a chance to do some really cool things, but honestly, Mom, I don't miss anything about L.A. right now. All I need is right here. You, Stevie—I mean, Steve," Mike corrects himself and smiles again, "Pops. I really enjoyed seeing Lisa again. Who knows? Maybe it's better timing."

"Oh, Mike. I'm so happy to hear that you missed

us and you're glad you came back. I'm especially happy to hear that there may still be something between you and Lisa. She's a special person, Mike. Just take your time. There's no hurry.

"Your Grandfather couldn't show it much, but he sure enjoyed seeing you. He has changed a lot, too. After your grandmother passed away, he's been in kind of a funk. I know he regrets how he treated her; she was his one and only." His mom nudges his foot with hers, a wink in her voice, "Maybe like you and Lisa?"

"The war took away so much of the man he was before he went to 'Nam. Some of the stories he would tell me about his time overseas were unimaginable. The things our country asked those young kids to do are just so unbelievable.

"Walking for hours or days through swamps not knowing if you would live to eat the next meal. Leaving behind the bodies of your best friends, killing other humans because they could kill you first. Most of the men were barely out of high school.

"I remember the summer before he left, I was five, it was so hot that Dad said he could fry an egg on the sidewalk. I didn't believe him, so he grabbed an egg from the refrigerator and told me to follow him. I'll be damned if that egg didn't fry just like he said it would. I thought he was the smartest person on Earth."

Jan's gaze points toward the fireplace as she

remembers. With a tilted head and a slight smile, she remembers another pleasant day.

"Running through the sprinklers was my very favorite thing to do on a hot summer day. Dad would connect the hose to the spigot and drag it to the middle of the yard. I would jump through the water for what seemed like hours. My dad would laugh and chase me, getting drenched right along with his girl." As her smile fades, Jan turns to look at her son.

"Then one day, he was gone. It took so long for him to come home and my mom was sad and scared every day. Dominic and I tried our best to be good and not cause any more grief, but we were so young. It was hard not to be just as sad as my mom."

"I never heard you talk so much about Pops. He was totally different when he came back, wasn't he?"

"He was, Mike. Like an absolutely different person. He wasn't fun, didn't smile, wouldn't run through the sprinkler, or read stories to us. He wouldn't even touch my mom. They used to be so huggy and kissy that Dominic and I would tease them.

"My mom started to pick fights and constantly nagged him until he left for good. At least, that's the way I saw it; Dad said it was his fault she was on his case all the time. But then my mom met someone else and, six months later, we had a new dad.

"This dad wasn't fun or nice or loving to me, but he seemed to enjoy his time with Dominic. They spent time doing outdoor activities; they built a fort in the backyard and would spend hours out there. They watched movies and played board games and baseball until one day Dominic wouldn't come out of his room.

"He said our step-dad touched him, but my mom said it wasn't nice to lie." Tears form and roll down Jan's cheeks before she has a chance to wipe them away.

"Mom, did someone hurt Dominic? Did he ever...hurt Sam?"

"Oh, Michael, all little boys tell fibs...who knows what was real?" Jan stands, picks up Mike's mug, even though he wasn't finished with his drink, and walks to the kitchen.

After all these years, Jan still kicks herself for not taking action when Sam told her that Dominic touched him. She had hoped that she would never have to admit that she knew. Never one to show much emotion, she sets the mugs into the sink, leans on the counter, and hangs her head.

That was odd. Did Dominic really touch Sam? Mom is obviously uncomfortable talking about it. I wonder why. Did she really know about the abuse with Danny? Was Uncle Dominic obvious about what he was doing with little boys? I can't remember anything that was 'off' looking back. Well, I guess he did hug too long and touch too much, but I thought that was normal for family.

Snow flurries speckle the sky outside Lisa's living room window and Mike remembers that California is a million miles away. Last year at this time, Mike invited Saul and Lisette to join Rebecca and him aboard a forty-foot yacht they were considering as their next large purchase; they took a three-hour sunset cruise in the Pacific.

By the time they returned home, a decision was made to compare other yachts before spending ten million on something they would only use a handful of times each year.

Landscape photographs, enlarged and framed, line the walls of Lisa's quaint home. Above the fireplace is one picture taken from "their" rock: a gorgeous view overlooking Oakdale.

Mike asks "Where did you find a photo of Oakdale taken from our rock? I thought we were the only ones who ever went there. The colors are fantastic. I've only seen the sky like this a handful of times."

"The photographer is a local woman who grew up in Oakdale. She is the President of the local photography club. Story is that this specific photo was taken when she went to this place to reminisce about her high school sweetheart after she found out that his best friend had taken his own life."

Mike tilts his head and turns to Lisa. "You?"

With a nod she explains, "I went there to think after I heard about Danny. The sky was perfectly painted; it was like he sent me a signal. The peace that filled my heart on that day let me know he was okay and that he is with us. Always."

"THANKS SO MUCH FOR LUNCH, Lisa. I have never had a gourmet grilled cheese before. Where did you come up with this idea? And the soup, oh, my gosh, was to die for. What is your secret?"

Heat rises to Lisa's cheeks and she is instantly thankful that her makeup covers the flush. "Oh, Mike. You're welcome. It's nothing, really. Just a collection of my favorite thing: cheese."

Dishes clink together as she lowers them into the sink before turning to Mike. "The soup's secret ingredient? Wouldn't be secret anymore if I told you, now, would it?" Eyes sparkle through a smile meant to tease.

"I might have to join a gym. This southern cooking is going to fatten me up. You know, you and my mom should really get together. She took a class with Paula Dean and puts her own spin on everything from fried chicken to meatloaf." The grin on Mike's face is so natural he doesn't realize how long it has been there until his cheeks start to ache.

"I have to admit that my latest hobby is trying new recipes and adding a touch of me to make them unique. This tomato soup, for instance, has cream cheese in it! Oh, no. Now, I might have to kill you." Lisa smirks, raises an eyebrow, and lets out a chuckle.

"Jan is so lucky; Paula Dean is one of my favorite chefs. I would give anything to have a class with Jacques Deveraux, though. He is my absolute all-time favorite. His cookbooks gave me the inspiration to start creating my own recipes." Lisa's eyes glaze over thinking about the fantasy of meeting Jacques and she shakes her head to come back to the present.

"Enough about me. What's your favorite hobby these days, Mike?" With an elbow on the dining room table, Lisa settles her chin in her hand.

"Wow, that's a hard question. Between managing the bars and attending fundraisers, I really don't have time for a hobby. Unless you count listening to new and unique musical acts.

"I absolutely love hearing a voice that doesn't sound exactly like Britney Spears or Tim McGraw or a guitar riff that is different than Slash or George Lynch. It seems like most people try to emulate their idol instead of finding their true identity."

"I would count that as a hobby; it's something you love." A genuine smile spreads across Lisa's face.

"Speaking of something I love; do you have any ideas on what I can do to help Steve? There has to be a way to reach him before it's too late. We had quite the confrontation yesterday." Mike leans back in his chair and crosses his arms. "He hit me, Lisa."

"Mike," Lisa's gasp is cut off by a wave of Mike's hand.

He shares the entire story and ends with "I think he overheard us talking from the top of the stairs. Mom and I were discussing Sam and how his bad choices led to his current situation. She said that she sincerely hopes Steve isn't taking that same path.

"You and I both know that my brother has let down his entire family from how he has decided to live his life. The drug addiction started out as a choice and if he ever changes his ways, that will also be his choice. I'm not sure how much you and my mom have discussed this, but I can assume you've been told a fair amount about how Sam got to where he is."

"Yes, your mother and I have had quite lengthy discussions about Sam and how his living situation affects his son. When Steve's mom disappeared, Sam spiraled into the most unlikely lifestyle any of us could have imagined. Homelessness is usually a temporary situation and family plays a very important role in healing those with a mental issue.

"Sam rejected any attempts to remedy his problems and made the decision that Steve would be better off without him. I know you have already heard all of this from your mom but coming from my point of view may be able to help you see a way that Steve can benefit from your presence.

He needs a male adult, a good role model in his life. Someone that can teach him how to be a strong man and make good decisions. Now more than ever, I think it's really important for you to build a healthy, stable relationship with him."

Not always Mike's strong suit, he listens intently as Lisa explains her interpretation of how Steve's feelings have influenced the outcome of his actions. Viewing his friend across the table, the affection and empathy in her eyes are unmistakable. Lisa genuinely cares for Mike's nephew, not just as a student but as a vulnerable human.

"Can you tell me how Steve's classmates have treated him? How they reacted to his dad becoming homeless and Steve having to live with his grandmother? What do they say to him? What words made him react with violence? What do I need to know about his daily activities away from home?" The oak table creaks as Mike leans forward on his elbows, eager to hear Lisa's response.

She takes a moment to think, inspecting Mike's face for an indication of how he'll react to her words. "This isn't going to be easy to hear," she starts. "Your mother tried her best not to cry when I filled her in on each altercation," Lisa pauses, closes her eyes, inhales, then exhales releasing pent-up anxiety before she continues.

"Before the first fight, Sam came to the office looking for Steve. He was drunk and belligerent, demanding that he see his son. The office called security and they literally threw Sam out the front doors of the school and threatened to call the authorities if he ever came back.

"This happened during the most inopportune time of the day. The lunchroom was filled with students that had just sat down for their lunch period. Steve had seen the scuffle from the hallway.

"One of the boys that used to be friends with Steve before Sam...well, he was the one who told all the kids in the lunchroom that Steve's dad is a homeless drunk. If I remember correctly, he said *'No one wants you, Steve. Your mom ran away and your dad is a drunk. I bet your grandma cringes every time she looks at you.'*

An audible groan escapes from Mike, but he does not interrupt.

"Steve lost it and just started wailing blindly. He threw punches at the air, mostly. It was a devastating loss, Mike. Just horrible. Steve walked away with a bloody nose and black eye." A tear leaks down Lisa's cheek as she remembers the scene.

"Sam stayed away after that. The next two times he was in a fight, I wasn't there to witness them, but I heard that they started the same way, older boys teasing Steve for his family life, but they ended differently. Steve connected punches and grew more confident.

"He has hardened and it shows in his work. Other teachers have commented on assignments he completes. In English class, he wrote a paper about leaving society and living in the mountains alone. In his art class, he drew a picture of a homeless person slumped against a wall in an alley with blood dripping off his clothes.

"Your mom has taken him to counselors for someone to talk to and I think it's helped, but he really needs a father figure in his life. Someone to help guide him and to support Jan, as well. You asked what you can do; you can be you. A loving, gentle, empathetic, kind uncle. He needs you, Mike."

Shaggy blond hair falls in Mike's eyes as he gazes at the table, thinking. His head nods over and over as his fingers rub the scruff on his chin. When he raises his eyes to Lisa, he runs his hand through his hair, composing himself before he speaks.

"Do you have other plans for today?"

"What? Um, no. That's not the reaction I

expected."

"Yeah, sorry," Mike smirks. "I think I have heard enough to process all this, and I need to do that alone, but not now. Let's change gears; I would really enjoy spending more time with you. Do you want to go for a drive?"

BLACK PAVEMENT SHOWS through a light dusting of snow. Jan's Buick SUV is four-wheel drive and Mike grew up driving these mountains during all types of weather, so Lisa is not nervous.

She is a bit surprised when Mike pulls into the parking lot of their overlook—the place where they spent so many hours making out during the beginning of their relationship.

During the winter months, this also became their favorite place to climb into the backseat. Lisa's face flushes at the memory of their better days.

Mike eases the Buick into Park before turning to Lisa. "Yeah, good times, eh?" With a wink from her old love, a giggle escapes her throat, and she is taken back to when she was seventeen. His hearty laugh conveys that he can feel her energy and agrees with a nod.

"Lisa, this place holds so many of my best memories. The times I spent here with you and with Danny. He and I used to come up here to get away from both our parents. When the Falls were frozen, we brought a six-pack or a bottle here.

"We had the best talks and made decisions about our lives." Mike's face changed from a smile, flattens before he turns to gaze out the windshield.

"I have so much to process from the last few days. Steve, Sam, Danny. You." As his thoughts trail off, Lisa fills the silence.

"You haven't talked about Danny and I didn't want to bring it up out of context or if you weren't ready, but Mike, I hope you know how sorry I am. He was one of my best friends, too. After you left, we saw each other a few times when we were both out and about, but it just wasn't the same."

With pursed lips, Mike nods and opens the car door; Lisa follows his lead. Her wool coat wraps around her as she tugs it closer and pulls gloves over her fingers. Crisp cool air and a scent of pine reach Lisa's senses. Tree branches stretch over the path that leads to their favorite rock. Mike moves them out of the way for Lisa to pass through the space.

"I was just here a couple nights ago. Saturday, after lunch with Mr. and Mrs. Jones, I was drawn here. It was almost as if Danny called me to our spot. Lisa, can I tell you something?"

"Of course, Mike. What's on your mind?" Granite rises out of the ground to form a perfect bench. Lisa and Mike spent so much time in this spot that they claimed it as 'their' rock. Mike spreads a blanket over it to protect them from the cold. Confused, Lisa didn't see it in his arms as he got out of the SUV; maybe she wasn't paying attention.

"Danny's parents shared his last words with me in the form of a letter." In the brief pause, Lisa raises her hand to her mouth and forces herself to be quiet.

"He explained something that I find completely profound, unimaginable, inconceivable. I just..."

"Mike," Lisa touches his arm. "I'm here. You're safe with me, you know that, right?"

As he blinks, Mike nods and continues. "My uncle Dominic molested him." Searching Lisa's expression to gauge her reaction before saying anything else, he is relieved when she grips his hand and turns to face him.

Staring into his eyes, she nods and says a simple "okay" with a shaky voice. Mike shares what happened during the visit with Danny's parents, how his mom appeared so strong, even though he knew she was dying all over again, and how he hasn't said anything to anyone. "I really want to tell my mom, but she doesn't need any more stress, right now.

"At this point, I almost feel like it's gossip. I don't think I have completely processed the entire situation yet." Snow blankets the side of the mountain and Mike is silent for so long that Lisa thinks he might just be counting each flake. "Some say my uncle was a good man, but Lord, I think he sinned."

"I don't know what to say. It doesn't feel like

anything would be appropriate. Mike, I'm sorry." Dark hair falls over her shoulder as Lisa tilts her head and repositions herself to be in Mike's line of vision. "Mike. Will you please look at me?"

He turns to her with tears streaming down his cheeks. Lisa wraps her arms around Mike's shoulders and allows him to bury his face in her chest.

Strong shoulders shake as Mike cries, again, for his lost friend and what Danny had to deal with—the pain he bore for so long alone. Standing tall, Mike changes positions, so he can hold his girl as he had so many years ago. They cling to each other in shared sorrow until they are too cold to stay outside.

HEAT RADIATES through the leather seat and warms Lisa's body, but not her heart. She can't shake the image of a teenage Danny in the sick sights and clutches of the small-town preacher. Dominic had been a respected member of the community and one of the people that would always lend an ear or suggest ideas on how to solve any problem.

New parents would reach out to him for advice on how to get their child to sleep through the night, newlyweds would ask about money problems, and the elderly often sought out answers on how to trust their doctor. Whatever the question, Dominic always had a reasonable and acceptable solution.

"These heated seats are awesome, Mike. Your mom must love this SUV and it's so stylish; even when money was tight, she found a way to keep up with the latest trends. Remember the Mink she found at an estate sale? She wore it everywhere, even to the grocery store." Soft material supports Lisa's head as she relaxes into the comfortable seat. "Hey, Mike?"

"Yeah?" Lost in his own thoughts, Lisa brought Mike back to Earth.

"It may not be my place to ask, but what's the situation with your marriage?"

After releasing a long sigh, Mike turns to Lisa. "Without going into a ton of detail, it was never what I imagined marriage would be. It was never true love, more of a convenient partnership. She needed a rich man; it looked better for me to have a beautiful bride. Win, win, right?" He sighs. "I don't love her, never have." He says this without malice, just a simple statement describing what he now saw as something more like a business transaction.

"I see." Perplexed, Lisa stares at Mike through squinted eyes, he isn't sure how to read her thoughts.

"I'm really sorry, Lisa."

"For what?"

"For the way we left things. I've never really apologized to you. I am truly sorry." Mike's warm fingers squeeze Lisa's hand as he searches her eyes.

"Things could have been so different if I wasn't such an asshole. God, I loved you. Do you know that you made every day of my life worth living? I remember the first time we kissed, I got butterflies. I never told you that. When you looked into my eyes, I felt what you felt; it was like we were connected. When it was good, God, it was great, but man when it went bad...

"I've never had that feeling with Rebecca. Maybe I closed myself off on purpose. It hurt so much when you broke up with me, I never wanted to feel that kind of pain again. If it weren't for Danny, I would have lost my ever-loving mind, I swear. Or drank myself to death. He kept me moving and took my mind off you in ways that the bottle couldn't."

"Oh, Mike. I wish we could have had this conversation back then," Lisa touches Mike's cheek. "We were going in such different directions; it was inevitable that we had to be apart. Life was totally different once we weren't kids, anymore. When we lost..." Lisa's voice fades at the memory.

"The baby." Mike finishes her thought. "I used to think about it every day. How things would have been if we stayed together and raised a child. Honestly, so many years later, it almost seems like a blessing. Please don't hate me for saying that."

Lisa smiles with warmth. "I don't, Mike. It wasn't the right time. God truly does work in mysterious ways. Do you remember your drunken proposal the night we broke up? I was so sad and I knew you would have done anything to make me stay."

Mike's long fingers tuck a strand of hair behind Lisa's ear. "You knew we didn't have a future if I was going to stay at Red's and never leave this small town. You had so much more faith in me than I ever did. All the dreams I had for my future ended up at the bottom of every bottle until you left. I should thank you for being strong enough to know what was best for both of us.

"Sometimes I wonder how things would have been different if Gene didn't die. Would you have come back to me? Would Danny still be alive? Would my brother be homeless? Would Stevie hate me?"

Their eyes lock in an exchange of emotion; both fall into a comfort that they only feel with each other. As their bodies seem to move without thinking, they lean closer over the center counsel. "I've missed you, Lisa," Mike whispers before his lips brush hers for a brief moment.

Scruff tickles Lisa's chin and she moves back with a shy smile. Mike's hand raises to her cheek and she leans into him.

"As much as I would love to spend the entire day with you, I have to go see my dad. I'm sure you have things to do, too," Mike says.

Lisa nods in agreement.

"Listen, tomorrow is New Year's Eve. If you don't have any plans, I would love to spend more time with you. Will you do me the honor?"

Chapter 9
DECEMBER 30, 2014

Harriman Imports is located on the south side of Roane St, south of the city. Ronnie Higgenbottom chose this location because the lot is between a Chevrolet dealership and a Dodge dealership. Customers looking for high-class vehicles for the first time sometimes start with the well-known brands before they realize speed and looks are only half of the experience.

Corvettes and Challengers are fast and fun but don't offer the luxury that most buyers desire. Once they figure that out, all they need to do is walk next door to find more options. Ronnie is more than happy to introduce these potential buyers to classy alternatives.

Lexus and Audi built their dealerships closer to the city and only sell about half of the vehicles compared to Harriman Imports.

Paperwork covers Ronnie's desk in an organized mess. He doesn't typically close deals himself, but the top two sales associates are on vacation over the holidays. Once the young, rich couple finishes signing their forms, he walks them to their new Porsche.

Ronnie is pleased to have another customer waiting in the showroom. Behind their backs, the sales team calls their loyal customers schmucks; the rich rarely haggle over prices making it easy to sell overpriced warranties and accessories.

ALL RIGHT, *Danny. Let's find out what my dad did with the million I invested to upgrade his dealership. Think he has any exotics? I would love to take a Ferrari or Bugatti out for a spin.*

Mike chuckles at the memory of doing donuts in the high school parking lot with a brand-new Camaro his senior year. If his dad had found out, he and Danny would have certainly been punished. Severely.

Vibration accompanies a segment of Madonna's "Vogue" interrupting Mike's thoughts. From the ringtone, he already knows it's Rebecca and unfortunately, he knows this conversation needs to happen for both of them to be able to move forward.

No time like the present.

"Hey, Bec. I told you I would be home next Sunday. Is there something you need?"

"Mike! My God, what is happening with you? I'm

freaking out! Last thing I knew, we were going to plan a vacation with the Goldman's and all of a sudden, poof, you're gone. You won't answer my calls..."

"How's your friend, Joe?" Mike interrupts his wife. The even cadence of Mike's voice is typical when he confronts Rebecca.

"What? Joe who? Mike, have you lost your mind? Did Hickville fuck up your brain?"

Mike holds the phone away from his ear and looks around the parking lot to be sure customers can't hear Rebecca's squawks through the window. "Joe who? How quickly you forget. You know, the senator that you were riding in the Friedman's study?"

Silence.

"No response. Ok. You're making this easy. We're through. I'm done putting up with your lies and deceit. You have until next Sunday to pack your shit and leave my house. Is there anything else, Bec?"

"But..." Panicked, Rebecca tries to lie her way out of another sticky situation. "Michael, you don't understand."

"I don't understand that I saw you fucking the senator, just like I must have had a hallucination last month when you were naked in the pool? I saw someone jumping the privacy fence, Rebecca. Tell me, was that Joe or one of your other 'friends'?"

"Please, let me explain..."

Mike interrupts her, finished with the games. "Goodbye, Rebecca."

Before exiting the car, Mike takes a few seconds to recoup. When Rebecca is on a roll, it's exhausting to talk with her.

Danny, can't you find a way to haunt Bec, so she'll leave me alone for a day? Just one day, that's all I'm asking. I told her I would be home next Sunday; it's only Tuesday. Jesus, woman, just go away already.

I'm so over her phony façade. She lies about every aspect of her life. Her closest friends don't even know how she slept her way into modeling, or that she spent 30 days in rehab just before we met. She's so good at fooling everyone in her life that she should have been an actress, really.

You should show yourself to her as a semi-transparent entity when she's in the middle of entertaining one of her "friends" and totally freak her out. I would laugh my ass off! Oh, God, I would give anything to play some sick prank like that on her. Would serve her right.

HEAVIER THAN THE last time Mike saw him, Ronnie buttons his suit jacket as he leads a potential customer out the front door to a 2015 Porsche 911 GT3.

Not making himself obvious, Mike exits the Buick near the main doors and enters the showroom where he begins to browse. A BMW X6 grabs his attention; jet black on black is Lisa's favorite.

She was impressed with Mom's Buick; I can't imagine how

she would react to a vehicle three times more luxurious. Not only does this have heated seats, but it also has air-conditioned seats for those super-hot summer days when your legs stick to the leather.

As he straightens his tie, Ronnie clears his throat and heads over to the guy who parked the Buick in the front row. "Can I help you find your dream car, son? That SUV is a real beauty. BMW has improved the performance dramatically over the years on this line."

Bent at the waist, inspecting the cockpit, Mike nods his head. "Mmm-hmm. They sure have." When he turns toward his dad with a smile, squinted eyes stare back at him for a split-second before Ronnie recognizes his son. It's been almost five years and Mike expects his dad did not anticipate him showing up in town, let alone at the dealership.

"Mikey? Oh, my God, boy. I didn't expect to see you here." A slap on the shoulder jars Mike; his balance thrown off; he side-steps. Ronnie grasps both shoulders and brings him to his chest for a tight hug before holding him at arm's length. "You sure don't look like California with that scruff on your chin. What brings you to Tennessee?"

"Hey, Dad. How the hell are ya?" Shaking off the tight grip, Mike rubs his face and explains, "Mom asked me to come home. Steve is going through a rough patch, so I thought I would come see if I could help out."

Metal under his hand warms and Mike peers at the BMW beside him. "I think I'm going to stay for a while and need some wheels. I can't borrow Mom's Buick forever."

Ronnie slips right back into sales mode and picks up on Mike's interest. "You sure you don't want something with more speed or sex appeal, son? Maybe something like a Porsche to pick up the ladies?" Eyebrows waggle and a smirk forms as Ronnie teases his son.

With a laugh and a shake of his head, Mike says, "you sure haven't changed have you, Dad?"

"Never." Ronnie winks and turns his focus to the BMW. "Well, let me tell you, son, this beauty is a top-notch, Grade-A, one-of-a kind, classy-ass specimen. Wanna take her for a ride?" Before Mike is able to answer, his dad steps toward his office and throws his voice over his shoulder. "I will have one of my guys open the doors to the showroom."

"THIS GORGEOUS GIRL is not quite an SUV. BMW owners don't want something much bigger than the old Z4. This X6 is a contradiction on the road: Her performance is more impressive than her hefty size. Can you believe she weighs almost 5,000 pounds?" The second he starts the vehicle, his dad starts selling.

How often has he practiced this speech? An Ad Exec could have drafted these words for a pamphlet...probably did. I bet he memorized the BMW catalog from beginning to end. Well, he should if that is his livelihood. Good for him.

"A twin, turbocharged V8 easily pushes this girl's mass. Can you believe she can hit 60 mph in 4.6 seconds? Even though it won't slice and dice like a 4 Series coupe, the X6 is comfortable for hours on everyday roads.

"In all-wheel-drive and with hill-descent control, she can crawl around steep terrain, but Mikey, let me tell ya, you cannot take this girl off-road."

Leather under Mike's fingers warms after Ronnie pushes a button on the dash. Soon after, his rear end starts to warm, as well. Smiling at his dad he nods an approval. "How much we talkin', Pop?"

"For you, son, I can let this beauty go for $98k. When do you want to pick her up?"

"I will give you $93k and pick her up in the morning." Mike has mastered the art of negotiation and Ronnie understands the air of confidence. He resists the urge to badger his son into a higher price.

"You're a tough cookie. I guess you got that from your old man." With a wink and a smile, Ronnie agrees on the price offered.

∼

NEON LIGHTS FLASH *Corona* in the window of Jake's Bar and Grill. Mike follows his dad to the stools at the end of the bar and acknowledges the man pouring a Michelob Light from the tap.

"Jake, this is my youngest." A glass clinks in front of Ronnie and he nods to the bartender.

"Nice to meet you, Mike. What can I get for you?" Jake asks as he wipes his hands on a towel.

"I'll have a Sam Adams, thanks."

A menu sits next to the draft beer in front of Mike. "Looks like you're quite the regular, here. Jake knows your beer of choice and, I assume, your life story since he knows my name."

Ronnie shrugs and gives Mike his most pitiful smirk. His son has guessed that most of his evenings start at this bar, in this seat, with this beer.

After a look at the menu, a few sips of beer, and some lighthearted catch-up conversation, Mike changes the subject. "Mom says Sam is living in a tent community behind the Home Depot. Do you know anything about that?"

Pursed lips hold back the honest answer. Ronnie decides to play nice since Mike has come home. "When she first found out, she called me. We hadn't spoken since the divorce and out of the blue, she reaches out. I knew she must be really pissed off or really desperate to call me.

"All I know, to answer your question, is that those

people are down on their luck. From what I hear, most of them are on drugs or alcoholics, but a few have serious mental problems.

"There have been a few stories of people getting irate and going off inside the Dollar General when they didn't have what they needed in stock or McDonalds when management suggested they actually pay for their food.

"Staffers from Ridgeview will pick them up and keep them for evaluation." Ronnie washes down the comment with a swig of beer, nods to Jake for a second, and asks Mike if he wants another.

"To be honest, Mikey, I think Sam may suffer from both of those aspects. I think the drugs he did when he was younger served a dual purpose: to help him fit in with the older kids at school and to mask his memories of abuse. Eventually, that led to his being more than just a druggie; I believe he has some underlying mental issues."

"Wait," Mike interrupts. "What abuse? You never hit us. Well, a spanking and a good tongue-lashing when we were kids, but...?" To get a better look at his dad, Mike squints and leans closer.

"Look, I haven't told your mom this, but her brother, your Uncle Dominic, came to the dealership a couple years back looking for Sam. When I asked why he was looking for him, Dominic blew up on me. Get that! A preacher man swearing in my face and saying he never touched anyone, all in front of a showroom full of potential customers.

"I was so confused; I had no idea what he was talking about until after we closed. I sat at my desk, closed my eyes, and only then did I remember your mom saying that Sam told her Dominic touched him when he was about nine."

Unable to meet Mike's eyes, Ronnie searches the bottles of liquor at the back of the bar and whispers, "I didn't believe her."

"Dad," Mike speaks after minutes of silence.

"I blew it off. I didn't believe that someone in my family would be," Ronnie looks over his shoulder before he mutters the one word he never expected to say, "molested." Tears gloss over Ronnie's eyes and he blinks them away.

"Mom hasn't said anything to me, but Danny's parents did. I had lunch with them on Saturday and they told me that Dominic had done the same thing to him."

Mike makes the decision to not go into great detail with his dad regarding Danny's death. No good can come from it.

"Right. I heard about Danny. I'm sorry, son. Real sorry." Pursed lips and a nod of the head confirm his statement. "That kid was such a goofball. You and he got into some real predicaments, didn't you? Not without Sam's guidance, I'm sure."

"The three of us really had some fun back in the

woods and out by the Falls, that's for sure." The full glass of Sam Adams chills Mike's fingers. "He loved our lifestyle, the simple life. The four-wheelers and motorcycles were such a thrill for Danny—all of us, really. Any chance we could be out back in those woods, we were exploring somewhere new.

"Remember that day Sam, Danny, and I went fishing up at the old McTaggert place? I was, what, fifteen? The second I saw that bear, I prayed to God, I would make it to my 16th birthday. I didn't even have my driver's license yet. Hadn't made out with a girl or gotten drunk. You know," Mike smiles wide, matching his dad's expression, "the important things in life."

"Lucky for the three of you, he didn't give you a good chase. That could have been a horrific event, for sure. When you first told me about that, I almost lost it, seriously. If something had happened to you boys," Ronnie's voice trails off and stalls before he adds, "ironic, huh? Back then I would give my life to save you, but now I can't figure out a way to help my oldest boy."

"Yeah, Dad. Me, too. So," Mike turns the conversation from schoolboy shenanigans to his brother's current situation. "Mom called you? How have y'all been since then? She seems really happy and acts as if she's in a great place."

"Don't worry, Mikey, I won't ruin that for her a second time."

"That's not..."

"We've worked out our major issues," Ronnie continues, not letting Mike interject. "Time seems to have been what was needed to let us be at a point where we can talk if we have to. Sam needs more than just your mom to worry about him and she needs to know she isn't the only one."

Amber liquid meets Ronnie's lips as he sips another drink. He pauses, smirks then takes another drink. "We could have been a really great team if we weren't so damn young when we got together. I was such an asshole and she was so passionate. A shame, really."

"We didn't have much, Mike, but didn't your mom and I provide a good life for you boys? We always had food, a place to live, and clean clothes. When we needed some extra cash, your mother sold crafts and cakes at the farmers market, do you remember that?

"Then I got the job at the dealership and the money seemed to literally flow into my hands. Who knew that selling cars would bring in so much cash? Not to mention pretty girls. Look," Ronnie turns to his son, "I never really said I was sorry for being a shitty dad."

"Dad," Mike tries to interrupt again only to be dismissed by a shake of Ronnie's head.

"Let me say this, please. It's my fault that you boys had such a hard time. I should have been a better husband. I made your mother miserable and it didn't help you or Sam to see how I treated her. Stupid fights over burnt dinners and how much to feed the horses could have easily been avoided if I just let shit go."

Based on his language, Mike realized his dad was feeling the liquid courage. "It's really good to see you, Dad."

ROSIE LOADS the dishwasher as Jan leans against the counter with a brownie in one hand. "Jannie, don't you ever stop cooking? I swear I have gained thirty pounds since I've been here." As she closes the dishwasher and dries her hands, Rosie accepts the wine glass from her friend and employer.

"Complaining?" Jan tilts her head and raises her eyebrows.

"Never. Now, tell me what's going on with that handsome son of yours." Like a teenager on the prowl, Rosie grins and wiggles her hips as she follows her friend into the TV room.

"Talking about me behind my back?" a deep, disembodied voice comes from the hallway.

The high-pitch shriek forces Mike to let out a hearty chuckle.

"Oh, dear. You can't sneak up on old ladies like that." Fingers spread across Rosie's chest as it rises and falls. "You're likely to give one of us a heart attack."

"Who you calling old?" Jan giggles and Rosie follows suit.

These ladies are having a great time; who am I to interrupt? I can wait to tell Mom about my time with Dad today. Eventually, she'll see the BMW and surely ask questions.

"Do y'all have New Year's Eve plans?" The floral pattern of his mom's wingback chair sinks under Mike as he settles into it with a fresh brownie in his hand. He strategically positions himself between them, so he can keep an eye on them both.

Rosie leans forward with her wine glass in hand. As she raises it toward the sky, she brags, "yours truly will be accompanying Mr. Jewel to the yearly Real Estate New Year's Eve Gala at the Crowne Plaza, Knoxville."

Mike's mom squeals like a schoolgirl. "Ooh, girl. Good for you, he finally asked!"

Red wine sloshes as glasses clink in a toast. "It's about time that man made his move."

A smile comes to Mike's face seeing his mom so happy.

Jan turns to him. "And what about you? Any plans with Lisa?" Her eyes widen in anticipation.

She may be even happier than I am about Lisa and I talking again. "I have something up my sleeve," Mike's smirk spreads.

"Well, Romeo, spill." Rosie is just as interested in Mike's agenda as Jan.

Laughter fills the room as Mike explains that they

will just have to wait until New Year's Day to hear if his plan pleases Lisa.

At the top of the stairs, Steve overhears the adults talking and wonders why the hell everyone is so frickin' jolly. His dad is homeless, out on the street, probably cold and hungry, these people sure aren't doing anything to help him.

Chapter 10
DECEMBER 31, 2014

L ight from the cell phone screen illuminates the cabin of the BMW indicating another missed call, the third in thirty minutes since leaving Herriman Imports. Who could be that desperate to reach him? Once he turns into Lisa's driveway, he researches the call history, concerned that maybe Jan was trying to get in touch.

Rebecca didn't leave a message and Mike is not about to return the calls. Today's plans are designed for absolute enjoyment.

Mike steps out of his new car and begins to walk the short distance to the house. Before he reaches the porch, the front door opens and Lisa steps over the threshold. With a backpack over one shoulder, she closes the door behind her and double-checks that it's locked.

Mike brushes Lisa's cheek with a kiss and a bristle of whiskers makes Lisa giggle.

"Hey, there," and "Good morning," overlap as genuine smiles don both of their faces for different reasons. Mike is anxious to spend more time with Lisa to see if the butterflies will stick around and Lisa is excited about their adventure. She has no idea what plans Mike has arranged for their New Year's Eve together.

"Ready to have a great day?" An elbow extends and Lisa grasps it to accompany Mike to the car.

"Absolutely. When are you going to tell me what we're doing? And why did I need a change of clothes? Ooh, did Coach get a new car? She's beautiful."

"Nope. This one's mine. Picked her up this morning."

"Jet black on black, my favorite. Your dad must have been extra happy to see you. His son comes home after five years and he makes a big sale."

After Lisa lowers herself into the passenger seat, Mike closes the door, turns to face away from her view, and reveals a huge smile. He doesn't want to give anything away too early, so he makes sure it's reduced to a grin before he opens his own door and slides into the driver's seat.

"You didn't answer my questions." Long brown hair falls over her shoulder as Lisa turns to confront Mike.

"That's true."

Lisa's interrogation efforts amuse him. She's cute when she doesn't know the entire plan. With an exaggerated exhale, an eye-roll, and a smirk, Lisa leans back to enjoy the warm leather seat.

God, she's gorgeous. I love nothing more than making her wait when I know she'll love what I have planned. She will be so excited when she finds out where we're going.

"Why are you looking at me like that?"

It's almost as if she can read his mind. Mike shrugs with fake nonchalance, teasing her.

"You're killing me, Mike Higgenbottom. God, you have not changed one bit." The fake glare pulls a hearty chuckle from Mike.

Gorgeous.

Of course, he had changed. A lot. Not only has he learned the value of a dollar and the importance of loving what you do, Mike appreciates honesty and friendship more than he had in the past. The true friends he has made in L.A. mean more to him than any artificial friends he made at Red's. Most of those guys were just in it for a free beer.

Mike is more patient than before and he enjoys making people smile. He feels the need to make Gene proud by donating large sums of money in his name.

LIKE A CROW ATTRACTED to shiny things, Lisa is pulled to the fancy controls of the BMW. She starts hitting buttons like she's playing a video game.

"What does this do?" As she presses the button, the sunroof starts to move, startling Lisa. "Oh!" Laughter rings like the whisper of angel wings in Mike's ears. "How do I stop it?"

Mike presses a different button to reverse the sunroof and smiles at Lisa. He made sure he knew the purpose of each button, knob, and plug before he left the dealership.

Lisa focuses on the large screen in the middle of the dash; options change from the AM/FM radio to the navigation system, bringing a smile to her face. Mike chuckles as he enjoys the simple country girl exploring a luxury vehicle. He almost forgot that most normal cars don't offer such amenities—at least, not the cars teachers own.

"Dual climate control, heated seats, very nice for bum-warming, by the way." Mike throws Lisa a wink and she blushes.

Leather squeaks under Lisa's jeans as she shimmies into a comfortable position. "Do you remember my favorite car back in high school? The Z3; not the Z4, I like the rounded look better. If I had my way back then, it would have been my sweet sixteen gift from my parents."

Unable to slow her rambling, she continues, "This

is so nice, Mike. I absolutely love it. You're so lucky. A backup camera, steering wheel controls; what else could you possibly ask for in a car? Oh, and the sunroof is awesome. I have always wanted one of those."

"Cooled seats, too, which is so great for the summer."

Lisa's eyes are like a kid on Christmas.

Mike nods, confirming. "Awesome, right? XM radio, USB ports, and park assist are pretty cool, too. My personal favorite is the steering wheel control options. You don't have to move your hands to turn up the volume or change the channel. You can even make a phone call with the press of a button." Mike laughs out loud when he glances toward Lisa to find her mouth open in awe.

"So cool. XM radio? I thought that option was only for ri…" Lips purse as Lisa stops herself from saying 'rich people'. She is in a brand-new BMW, after all. "What's your favorite channel?" Hoping Mike doesn't catch on to what she almost said, her face grows hot from embarrassment under her smile.

"I have already pre-set the stations I enjoy most. See what you think."

Lisa flips through the first three stations and listens for a few seconds before making a change. On the fourth station, she hears one of her new favorite bands, *Heaven Scent*. As Lisa sings along with their latest single, "Who Are You?" she dances in her seat, channeling her high school self, and Mike has a hard time keeping his eyes on the road.

Gorgeous, he thinks again.

"I just love this band. I love their message. All their songs are positive and encourage kids to be genuine, true to themselves, to stay in school. I read that this song was written when Charlie and Alli were in high school trying to figure shit out. Everyone told them they would never make anything of themselves and they strived so hard to prove the naysayers wrong. Such a great success story."

Lisa gushes, smiling at Mike as she talks about their music. "Charlie plays lead guitar and Alli is their lead singer; they're the founding members. They're from this small town in Michigan and pull from their past experiences for song ideas."

Mike loves how much Lisa knows about the band he discovered. She's adorable when she's in her element, talking about something she loves.

"Yeah," he says, "They are a couple of really nice girls; genuine, down-to-earth. I think together they keep each other grounded and humble. When they first started writing songs, they made a pact to be an uplifting band—writing more about self-love and confidence than relationships, for example. They write about how to become who you want to be, love yourself, never give up, don't back down..."

Lisa raises her eyebrows and tilts her head. "You say that like you know them."

With a smirk, Mike glances at Lisa. Her expression brings out a chuckle as he admits he knows the band. "I do. I discovered them a few years ago."

"Wait," with a shake of her head, Lisa squints, then turns to watch the scenery pass through her window as she thinks about how to pose the following question. "I know that you own a couple bars in L.A., but I never asked what that means. I thought it was just, you know…music and food. But it seems like maybe there's more to it?" After Lisa studies Mike's profile, she asks how he discovered *Heaven Scent*.

"When I first moved to L.A., I got pretty caught up in society, you know, parties and throwing money around. After I calmed down a little, I knew I needed to do something productive with my time. I figured out what I loved most and found a way to be successful. I knew I was good at managing a bar, just bad at drinking. When I bought my first bar in 2010, it had a stage.

"I knew right away that I wanted to have a place for up-and-coming musical groups to get their start. Remember how we always had to travel so far to hear good music? I turned the tables and brought good music to my customers. *Great* music.

"I named the place after Gene. God rest his soul." Mike's forearm warms under Lisa's touch.

"Oh, Mike, that's fantastic. Fascinating. How many groups would I have heard of?"

"Depends on what genre of music you listen to.

Gene's hosts rock bands while Lisa's has found more than a few country and pop stars. Sam's finds a way for more grunge and metal groups to get their start." With a smirk, Mike waits for Lisa's reaction.

"Lisa's?" She squints at him and nearly frowns.

Unsure if she was flattered or upset, Mike explains that the bars bear the names of the most influential people in his life. "Yes, Lisa. You are one of those people."

"Oh, Mike. That's so sweet. I'm honored." She touches his arm again. "Are those your only bars or are there more?"

"Just one more. Six months ago, I went in a different direction and opened a sports bar. Athletes from all kinds of sports come in and spend time with underprivileged kids in the area. My GM is an ex-football player and a really great guy. Coach's has been a huge success in the community."

"I'm so proud of you, Mike. You have found your niche."

WINGS of the Gulfstream extend from the side of the personal airplane like wings of an exotic bird, or a Pterodactyl. Once Lisa realizes that they are driving toward the jet, she asks if the aircraft belongs to Mike.

"It does."

"God, Mike, I knew you came into a lot of money

and people said you were rich, but…" Not able to find the right words, Lisa shakes her head and turns to Mike. "Really? Like *rich*, rich?"

"Yeah, I guess so." Uncomfortable with bragging about his means, Mike raises his eyebrows and fake grins, making Lisa giggle.

"Holy shit," Lisa responds under her breath. She had no idea the extent of her ex-boyfriend's wealth.

The door at the top of the stairs opens and a pilot greets the couple. "Good morning, Mr. Allen. Are you and your friend ready for your trip?"

"Trip?" Lisa's eyebrows raise as does her gaze into Mike's eyes. Again, smiles reach both of their faces. Wool separates Mike's hand from the small of Lisa's back as he leads her up the steps.

Vanilla scented spurts of air burst from the ducts strategically hidden behind the four rows of seats. Comfort and class were two of the things Mike desired most when searching for the perfect jet. Little things like scent provide an additional level of comfort, bringing a piece of home puts most people at ease.

"I can't get over this plane, Mike. This is just incredible. How great that you can get up and go anywhere at any time. I love it. No traffic, no crowds, no hassle. Ah, what a life you must lead."

Wood trim is smooth under Lisa's fingertips as she traces the edge of the table on one side of the plane. Eight seats line the front half of the cabin in front of an open area used for relaxing during long flights.

"Come sit while we take off; we'll be able to wander after we hit thirty thousand." Mike reaches for Lisa's hand like it was ten years ago and they never spent a day apart. Being with her is as natural as breathing. There are no uncomfortable moments, no awkward silences, no reason to deny the emotions.

"Mr. Higgenbottom, when will you be informing me of our destination?" Lisa's proper speech compels Mike to smile.

"Miss Johnson, that's for me to know and you to find out." He sticks out his tongue in true teenage fashion. "Not accepting that answer?"

Lisa shakes her head.

"Okay, how about this, then. Where we are going is a place I love and want to share with you."

"Fine," a bashful smile confirms her approval.

After they buckle in for lift-off, Lisa asks if he remembers Graduation Day. "The best day of our lives, up until that point. God, could we have been any happier? Our lives were just beginning."

"Your parents took so many pictures I thought my face was caught in a perma-grin, I swear. Your mom was always so supportive of us. So was mine. She still is."

Lisa smiles with ease as she listens to the rhythm of Mike's voice.

"Do you know how much she wants us to be together?" he asks.

"Yes, I do. She talks about you all the time. Can't say enough good, like she's bragging and wants me to be impressed. I'm not, by the way." Lisa never knew how hard it was to keep a straight face when she makes such an incomprehensible joke. Only able to keep up the charade for a second, her face shines with joy.

"My dad pushed me to 'sew my wild oats,' even though he absolutely thought you brought out the best in me. He wasn't the best role model for a faithful relationship. When you were taking classes in Knoxville, he was pushing me to date other girls. I never did, though. You know that, right?"

"I know," Lisa nods.

"That night your ex-boyfriend came into the bar and gave you shit…"

"And you came to my rescue and kicked his ass?"

"Yeah, that night." Mike's smile widens when Lisa touches his arm, again. "Well, when I saw my dad the next day and told him what happened, he wasn't as proud of me as I thought he would be. He shook his head and asked why I was wasting my energy on a relationship that wouldn't last."

Not expecting Lisa to frown, Mike forgot that she wears her heart on her sleeve. Impossible to hide her emotions, he remembers that he always knew how she felt about any situation.

"I was so afraid that he would press charges; it would be just like him. God, he was such a jerk in high school. Speaking of pressing charges, I remember when you and Danny got arrested and his dad fed you a line of BS about being on vacation so he couldn't get you out of jail." Laughter rings like music in Mike's ears.

"Wait. Line of BS? You knew he could have got us out but let us sit in jail overnight? You little shit." Those words prompt Lisa to laugh harder. "That was one of the worst nights of my life and you knew it was all a crock? Man, I'm such a schmuck."

"You have to admit, Captain Jones was brilliant. Kept you two hoodlums out of some serious trouble."

Mike reaches for Lisa's hand and his fingers stroke her palm as they had all those years ago. The pilot interrupts their conversation to announce that they have reached cruising altitude and that it is safe to move around the cabin.

Pleased that she doesn't let go of his hand, Mike unbuckles, nods to Lisa, who follows suit, and leads the way to the lounging area of the plane. After making themselves comfortable, Mike jumps into another story, this one about their favorite place to hang out with best friends.

"Hey, remember when we first took Gene to the Falls? We had known him for what, a couple months? Man, that guy just fit right into our little crew, didn't he? I'm still amazed at the connection we had."

Lisa smiles at the memory and she joins in reminiscing. "He was such a kind, decent person who was good at what he did and wanted to help everyone. I wasn't surprised when you asked him to join us that first time. He was ready to go, wasn't he? Always accepted any invitation; almost like he wanted to spend time with you, but not in a weird way.

"If I didn't know any better, I would think he was your long-lost older brother. But your mom is way too young for that." A giggle escapes and Lisa continues. "It was a Saturday and Gene was spending the weekend in town because he had some big meeting in Oak Ridge the following Monday. We met up with him at your parent's house, had breakfast, and took off on four-wheelers. He never complained about anything, did he?"

Mike continues the story. "His four-wheeler ran out of gas halfway to the Falls so I gave him mine and you scooted back so I could drive yours." Still caressing Lisa's hand, Mike adds a light squeeze and lowers his voice as he leans closer. "I can still feel your arms around my waist."

Cinnamon mixed with Creed tickles Lisa's senses. Memories of fun they had as a couple at the Falls rush back. "Gene told stories about his travels and how each city had an equally impressive neighboring small town, like Oak Ridge and Oakdale. He said he liked Oakdale best, said the people were so inviting and kind." With a deep breath and blinking away tears, Lisa smiles at Mike.

"Yeah. He also said we knew how to have the most fun." One eyebrow raises as he continues, "He's right, you know. Those were the best years of my life."

"Mine, too."

"You, Danny, my brother, all of my favorite people loved each other equally. We all had our little squabbles, but always recovered." Pursing his lips, Mike adds, "Until we didn't."

"That's all water under the bridge, Mike. You're here, now, aren't you?"

Chapter 11
DECEMBER 31, 2014

Pressure in the cabin changes, and the pilot announces that they have begun their descent; Mike and Lisa should return to their seats.

Through the window, a metropolis appears and Lisa gasps. "Mikey? Paris?" A smile spreads across Lisa's face and Mike doubts her eyes could open any wider.

"Oh, my God," Lisa squeals and bounces in her seat. If the seatbelt hadn't been fastened, she would have jumped up and down.

Mission accomplished.

"This is number one on my bucket list. How...when..." with a shake of her head, Lisa dismisses the questions that refuses to form on her tongue. After a few more 'oh, my God's she catches her breath and turns to Mike just long enough to say, 'thank you' and plant a short, hard kiss directly on his lips.

Her attraction to the city from the air mirrors Mike's attraction to the woman beside him. Lisa has no idea the effect that her kisses have on him.

Pleased that his surprise is successful, Mike leans back in his chair and closes his eyes. Each time Lisa touches him, his heartbeat increases and he finds it difficult to breathe.

Danny, it's going to be a great day. I can't wait until Lisa sees the next surprise. It's going to blow her mind. This is the best feeling; knowing that you're making the love of your life happy and giving her something she would never give herself.

"Love of your life?"…Oh, that explains the palpitations. I have to tell you, Buddy, that I honestly wondered, what the hell? Thought maybe I was having a heart attack. Guess I'm in love, aren't I? Huh…haven't experienced this in years.

LISA GRASPS MIKE'S hand as he helps her out of the limo. Hair falls down her back as she tilts her head up to take in the sight of the Four Seasons George V.

"I must be in heaven," Lisa whispers to herself, but Mike hears and angles his head down to hide a grin. His heart skips a beat and he regulates his breathing while placing a hand on Lisa's back to support her.

"Mike, this is too much…" she shakes her head and glances from the hotel to Mike and back again.

"Shh, *mon amour*. We're here to have a good time. That's all. Just enjoy the day. Please." With an arm around her shoulders, Mike pulls Lisa closer and places a kiss in her strawberry-scented hair. "Come on, let's freshen up before lunch."

Inside the foyer, Lisa allows her fingers to brush along the surface of an antique console table and she glances into the large mirror above it. She can hardly believe she is actually in Paris and flashes a smile at herself.

"This room is absolutely magnificent; just beautiful," Lisa says as she steps into the living room of the expansive suite. She admires a Louis Bellon landscape painting over the sofa and the fire dancing inside the *cheminée* in the wall that divides the living and dining rooms. A sense of comfort rushes over her as if she is at home.

The bellhop places their overnight bags in the bedroom and Mike thanks him with a few francs. Turning around twice, he looks for Lisa, only to spot her on the balcony.

"I can't believe we're here. I probably have a dozen little bruises from pinching myself. I'm so happy to finally have this opportunity. Thank you, so much for bringing me here." She wraps her arms around Mike's neck and he lowers his head to revel in Lisa's rose petal scent.

"Mon chéri, n'importe quoi pour vous (*anything for you, my love*)." Mike anticipates Lisa will kiss him and prepares for an intense embrace. The last thing he expects is for her to grab his hand, lead him into the bedroom, climb into bed, and jump up and down. Shadows on the wall follow Lisa as she bounces and giggles.

"It's tradition, Mike, remember? Every hotel room has to pass the bounce test!"

SAUCEPANS HANG FROM THE CEILING, and stacks of plates, bowls, and saucers line the shelves on the wall behind an over-sized grill. Stainless steel countertops gleam as they anticipate a classic French lunch. Lisa's jaw drops when Chef Jacques Devereaux turns to the couple.

His accented voice welcomes them. "Michael, such a pleasure. Who is this beautiful young woman on your arm?" Jacques walks toward them and reaches for Lisa's hand, kissing the back of it in greeting.

"Lisa, please meet Jacques Devereaux. Jacques, Lisa is a special friend from my past."

"Mike," the word catches in Lisa's throat and comes out as a whisper. She tries again, "Mike, this is Jacques Devereaux." With wide eyes, Lisa gazes at the man standing next to her.

"Yes, it is." An attempt to cover a smirk is unsuccessful. "Jacques and I met years ago in Los Angeles at a party of a common friend. I was searching for a cook and Jacques recommended an extremely talented young man who has been with me ever since.

"When we last spoke, I mentioned your love for food and unique cooking talent, so Jacques has arranged to prepare a meal with you, today. Go." Mike nudges a giggling Lisa toward his friend.

"This is surreal," Lisa mumbles as she follows Jacques to the kitchen.

Behind a half-wall disguised as a bar, Mike finds a stool and perches to observe as his love performs one of her favorite activities.

After only a few minutes, Lisa finds her rhythm and works in complete harmony with her idol. The synchronicity is like watching a dance; Jacques leads the aspiring chef as any great teacher does. A glass of red wine is placed in front of Mike and he sips as his admiration grows.

An hour later, a four-course meal is ready to begin sampling. Lobster bisque, as creamy and delicious as Mike has ever tasted, is savored by the trio while waiting for the next course to finish cooking.

At the signal of the timer, Lisa rises to serve a spinach souffle to the men in addition to the largest, most genuine smile she has ever presented.

Wine glasses are topped off, again, before Jacques and Lisa jointly serve Mike the main course: two classic French dishes, Ratatouille and Hachis Parmentier.

Three plates with mounds of zucchini, yellow squash, Japanese eggplant, and Roma tomatoes topped with balsamic vinaigrette are placed on the table. Fragrant onions, garlic, and herbs emanate from the dish.

In the middle of the table lies a baking dish filled with ground meat cooked in gravy and layered with mashed potatoes. Grated Parmesan cheese tops the dish and adds to the array of aromas.

"Lisa is a natural, Mike. If she dances as well as she cooks, you're a lucky man. She moves around the kitchen as if she's been a professional chef for years. I have some proteges who aren't as talented as this one." A nod and a wink follow the compliment.

Not one to easily embarrass, Lisa's cheeks turn a faint shade of pink. "Merci beaucoup. Je veux jouir," Lisa raises her spoon and Mike nearly spits out the bite of Ratatouille. Jacques fails to disguise a chuckle.

"Excuse me?" Mike raises his eyebrows at Lisa.

"I want to enjoy," Lisa repeats the phrase in English.

"Oh. Well, that makes more sense." Mike touches her arm and smirks.

"Lisa, I'm impressed you have learned the art of speaking French. However, that specific phrase is a bit tricky," Jacque explains with kind eyes. "I believe what you meant to say is 'je veux profiter'. The order in which you spoke, 'jouir' means orgasm."

Her hand covers her mouth as Lisa gasps. A

hearty laugh follows, allowing the three friends to continue the lighthearted conversation through dessert. Their chocolate mousse proves to be the smoothest, light, and airy dessert Lisa has created from scratch.

THANKFUL that she thought to charge her extra camera batteries, Lisa unpacks the Canon as she exits the limo. Jacques offers to take them on a personal tour of downtown Paris to walk off their meal. Arc de Triomphe is the first stop.

Although she could surely get used to this kind of travel, she's not sure how she feels about such extravagance. Mike asked her to enjoy the day, so she will honor his request.

Thirty minutes later, they are off to the next destination. Even though they only have a short time to explore, Jacques has managed to choose his vision of the perfect Parisian tour. Like an expert guide, the history is explained with great detail in a French accent that pulls Lisa's lips into a smile time and again.

Parc Monceau offers a beautiful nature walk with statues and pyramids thrown in for effect. "Mike, I'm absolutely blown away," Lisa's hand finds his as if they were seventeen, again. "Thank you so, so very much for this day."

As they slow their pace, Lisa turns to stand in front of her high school boyfriend and reaches for his other hand. He moves close enough that their coats touch and he leans his head toward hers. A smile fades to a smirk before her lips part to meet his.

One hand caresses Lisa's cheek as the other finds the small of her back. Mike's lips cover hers and he holds his breath in disbelief of the butterflies that return. After two more long kisses, Mike breaks the bond and rests his forehead against Lisa's.

"Jesus, you take my breath away. You're so beautiful, *mon amour*." Searching her eyes, he asks the question that has plagued him all day. "What's going on, here? Do you feel the electricity, too?" With his hand still on her cheek, Mike stares into the eyes of the woman he loves, hoping she feels the same.

"Yes, I do. And I think we're making up for lost time," Lisa smiles and adds, "I haven't been this happy in years, Mike. I've missed you so much."

The single tear is kissed away before Mike wraps his arms around Lisa, picks her up off the ground, and spins her in a circle. Laughter fills the surrounding area and they remember they are not alone. Ready to continue the tour, Jacques interrupts the couple.

In true tour guide fashion, Jacques explains the history of the Montmartre Cemetery. In the mid-18th century, the cemeteries of Paris had become overcrowded, creating unsanitary living conditions in the surrounding neighborhoods. In the 1780s, the city of Paris closed the Cimetière des Innocents and burying corpses within city limits was banned.

"In 1825, The Montmartre Cemetery was opened. Initially known as Cimetière des Grandes Carrières (Cemetery of the Large Quarries) referencing the cemetery's unique location, an abandoned gypsum quarry. During the French Revolution, the quarry was used as a mass grave."

Cemeteries hold a special place in Lisa's heart, not for any specific reason other than her captivation with headstones. While staying close enough to hear the history of the cemetery, Lisa roams the area, shooting three photos of everything that calls for her attention.

The possibility of capturing an image of a spirit drives her to visit unique burial sites; three pictures in a row eliminates any question of the photo's integrity.

In the fifth grade, Lisa learned of Paris in history class and instantly started dreaming of visiting France. The Sacre Coeur cathedral quickly made her top five locations to explore. Constructed at the highest point in Paris, the panoramic views of the city from the top of the dome are spectacular and she couldn't wait to experience the view for herself.

Not disappointed, Lisa absorbs the knowledge of the historic landmark and savors the time she is able to spend there. Jacques' explanation of the Basilica is immensely detailed and Lisa is mesmerized by the man's French accent describing the large pipe organ.

It reminds her of the years she spent watching her grandmother play the organ in church.

The next stop, Mulan Rouge, is beaming with tourists so Mike and Lisa must view the home from across the street. "Sorry, sweetheart, this one is just a drive-by. Too last-minute to get tickets, but I wanted to be sure you could see the building."

They exit the limo and Jacques explains that the home with the red windmill on its roof is best known for being the birthplace of the 'can-can' dance and that the original building burned down in 1915. Lisa remembers when the movie with Nicole Kidman came out in 2001 and how she longed to visit Paris.

"I must leave you, now," Jacques kisses Lisa on both cheeks. "It has been a pleasure, mon amour." To Mike, he says goodbye and winks an approval when Lisa's back is turned before walking away.

"And, just like that, he's gone. Quirky fellow. Jacques is a great guy and a really good friend. He would give you the shirt off his back if you needed it." Mike shakes his head as the distance between them grows. "A bit of an odd duck, though."

"I still can't believe I cooked with him." Lisa places her hand over her heart and exhales. "I stood next to my idol and created fantastic food. It's so different meeting the actual human being instead of watching a celebrity on TV. The experience was simply a dream come true. Thank you, so much, Mike."

After capturing a few photos of the windmill house, they were on their way to Palais Garnier, an Italian-style opera house, which is known for its detailed, opulent architecture.

As they visit another of Lisa's top five on her wish list, she can't help but admire Mike. He remembered all those conversations they had about Paris. She had thought her dreams would've been forgotten by him, but here they were together, exploring the city she'd always wanted to see.

Lisa thinks about the old Mike. Even if he'd had the means to get them here, she doesn't know if he would've selflessly guided her through the city like this, let alone set up a meeting with Jacques. The Mike she's with today is new to her but also so familiar in some ways, and his thoughtfulness surprises her in the best way.

The Phantom of the Opera became another event on Lisa's bucket list after Mike took her to see the movie on one of their dates. She loved the romance story and that the book was based on a true story, but the old Mike thought the concept was too unbelievable.

"Remember when we went to see The Phantom in Knoxville and I asked how a ghost could fall in love with a human and seriously expect her to love him back?" Mike reminisced. "I hope this tour makes up for me being an ass." He fluttered his eyelashes, teasing Lisa.

She faked a mean glare, then reached for his hand. "You've grown over the years; I'm impressed." Lisa kissed his cheek.

"I wish we could see the actual play, today, but that will have to wait until our next visit. Sorry," Mike said and kissed the back of her hand.

The hour-long tour of the building that premiered the Phantom of the Opera surpasses Lisa's expectations and overloads her senses. After a fresh battery, her camera can keep up with Lisa's desire to capture every detail.

"How can all this beautiful architecture hold so much negative horrible history?" Lisa wonders out loud as she and Mike follow other tourists around the Fontaine des Mers at Place de la Concorde. Known for being the largest square in Paris, it is also the site of many public executions.

"King Louis XVI and Marie Antoinette were both executed at this very spot. 'Off with her head!' What?" Mike's cheeky comment makes Lisa roll her eyes.

"Michael." Unable to hide her amusement, Lisa squeezes his hand. "You're something else." Soft lips brush against the back of her hand, giving her chills of delight. With a slow blink, a smirk, and a tilt of her head, Lisa waits patiently for Mike to kiss her lips.

Pressure on the small of her back encourages her to inch closer. Lisa gazes into Mike's eyes as he lowers his head. As they embrace, everyone around them, along with the noises of voices and traffic, seemingly disappears and they enter their own world.

Staring into her eyes, Mike asks how Lisa feels before glancing at the hands of his Rolex for the time. "It's eight o'clock. Are you ready for dinner? Or do you need to go back to the hotel, first? You still look incredible, by the way. Just beautiful." A kiss confirms Mike's statement.

"I'm good to go; exhausted but exhilarated. I am hungry, though. We haven't been to the Eiffel Tower, yet. Are we going to be able to see it?"

"Of course." Grasping her hand, Mike winks and leads her to the limo.

THE JULES VERNE restaurant on the second floor of the Eiffel Tower offers a seven-course dinner. After Lisa and Mike are seated, they order a bottle of wine and relax into their chairs. Unable to release their hold of each other's hands, the couple rests their forearms on the table.

"What a day. Wow, we packed so much into the last six hours. What was your favorite place?"

"How could I possibly choose a favorite? Every single thing about this entire day has been surreal. After high school, I started saving every penny I could; you remember. I never quite found the time to make the trip. I still can't believe that we're here."

Lights of the city reach the infamous tower, which provides the iconic scene of the most popular postcards. Stars flicker in the sky surrounding a half moon.

"This view, what can I say, is pulled straight from my fantasies. Each of the places we visited today had a special meaning that I will never forget. Having explored the city of my daydreams for as long as I can remember with the person in that fantasy means the world to me. I could not have planned a better day."

Mike smiles at her and assures, "There is so much more to see. I absolutely love Paris and come here as often as I can. We'll need at least two weeks next time."

This promise to bring Lisa back to this city brings a smile to her face.

"The Louvre is too touristy and takes too much time to experience in a rush. I will arrange for a private tour when we come back; that's the only way to really appreciate everything there.

"To see the Palace of Versailles, the Hall of Mirrors, and the Salon de la Guerre, you need an entire day. They offer half-day trips, but I like to really explore the expansive gardens and Marie Antoinette's Royal Apartments. Oh, and Monet's House, too. There's just so much I want to experience with you, Lisa." A squeeze from his hand makes her grin.

"I would absolutely love that. I want to see it all. I have to say, though, that cooking with Jacques today must be the best experience I have ever had in my life. Being able to create a dish not only in front of or beside my idol but in conjunction with him. The best, seriously.

"Every single place we went, today, each time I took a picture, I fell more and more in love with this city. I don't know how I can ever thank you enough for what you have done for me, Mike. I just..."

Lisa pauses and gazes deep into Mike's eyes, tilts her head, and smiles genuinely. "I just fell in love with you all over again." She lets out a surprised breath and blushes. "Oh, I just said that..."

Her words are cut short by Mike's mouth pressing against hers.

"JE SUIS TELLEMENT PLEINE," Lisa tries her hand at speaking French again as she leans back in her chair and places a hand on her stomach. Mike doesn't hold back his laugh.

"I think you meant to say that you are full, but the words that came out didn't quite mean that. *J'ai trop mange* means I ate too much."

A sigh prefaces an eye-roll. "I'm sure you're going to tell me I said something embarrassing again, aren't you?"

"I sincerely hope you are not pregnant."

"Oh!" Lisa throws her head back allowing a loud

laugh escape. "Jacques is right; this language is tricky. You and I took French together in high school, but I don't remember being taught these phrases that can easily be confused. How did you become so fluent?"

"The chef that Jacques introduced me to, Andre, only speaks French when he sees me, which is basically every day. I hired him practically on the spot; he's fantastic. At first, I hated that he would rarely speak English, but once I let myself learn more, I began to insist we only speak French. He says it's his way of helping me improve."

Explosions followed by expanding colorful displays in the night sky startle Mike and Lisa laughs a little too loud. "How did so much time pass? It's dark already. Ready for a show?" Mike stands and reaches for Lisa's hand.

"Can we walk out on the balcony?"

"You bet." He leads Lisa to the terrace and she walks to the railing as if she's going to lean over to get a better look. "Mike, this is gorgeous, absolutely the perfect night to end a perfect day."

Muffled rock music begins to play and Lisa cocks her head trying to determine its origin.

"May I?" Palm up, Mike reaches for Lisa's hand, pleased with her honest smile. "Remember this?" Lifting his arm, he flicks his wrist, and Lisa twirls closer. Once she is secure in his arms, he sways his hips and moves his feet to the sound of their song from high school. Aerosmith's "Don't Want to Miss a

Thing" plays from Mike's phone, only loud enough for their ears.

After the song ends, Mike positions himself behind Lisa, wraps his arms around her, and places soft kisses on her hair. Red, white, and blue fireworks light the sky.

"I never stopped loving you, Lisa," he whispers in her ear.

She nestles closer in response.

Chapter 12
JANUARY 1, 2015

A bottle of French wine from the Clos De Belleville vineyard that Mike and Lisa visited earlier in the day sits half-empty on the table in front of Jan. She fills her glass for a second time and pours a glass for Mike. "Please join me for a drink, Mike. We need to talk."

Oh, boy. The 'we need to talk' line is never good. Mixed with two glasses of wine...even worse. The only time Mom has more than one glass of wine is when something heavy weighs on her mind.

After Mike takes a seat across from his mother, she slides the glass to him and nods. "I want to hear every single detail of your trip with Lisa. I just adore that girl and I am absolutely certain that your time in France was beyond fantastic, but I hope you don't mind if we talk about it later."

Jan hesitates with an extra-long sip. "Mike, this is

not a conversation that I ever wanted to have. With anyone. Ever." A deep breath and long exhale give Jan time to stall.

"Rip off the Band-Aid, Mom." Mike reaches across the table and touches his mom's forearm as he offers a sympathetic grin, hiding his concern. "Whatever this is about, we can work through it together."

"It's about Sam. I have kept his mental state close to my heart because I can barely breathe when I remember the look on his face when he told me about Dominic." Red liquid fills their two glasses, finishing the bottle off and Jan meets her son's gaze.

"I'm listening," Mike reassures her.

"When Sam was nine, he came home from youth group later than usual one night. You weren't old enough to attend, yet, so for once, the two of you weren't together. My brother picked him up and brought him home each Sunday evening.

"On this specific day, Sam was not his normal jovial self. He was quiet and his eyes were red and puffy like he had been crying. When I asked why he was so sad, he shook his head and ran to his room.

"It took a good three days before he opened up to me. When he finally told me what happened, he said that your Uncle Dominic showed him a new game and that he didn't want to play it again. Dominic said that if he didn't play, God wouldn't love him anymore.

"He burst out crying and jumped into my arms. Between sobs, he said that it hurt to go poop." Jan's hand covers her mouth as she replays the video in her mind. Tears well in her eyes and Mike squeezes her fingers, listening.

"Your dad was the one who totally blew me off when I explained what Sam had said. He belittled the very idea that our son was being abused. He said, *'Who would do that? Your brother, seriously? Jan, he's the town preacher. Think about it; that's just ridiculous. Besides, that could never happen to our boys.'* Your dad and I were never the same."

"Mom, I didn't know."

"How could you, dear?" Jan stares at Mike with eyes full of affection. "The next day, your dad came home with bloody knuckles and Sam never said another word about Dominic. Never acted sad like that day again. Your dad and I made a deal that we would never let either of you near my brother again. Ever.

"There wasn't really much that we could do because there was no real proof on our end. Just a nine-year-old boy's word versus a preacher; you know the trouble your brother used to give us. If we reported Dominic, who would believe us over the town preacher?"

"That's why we didn't attend his church," Mike frowns as he begins to connect the dots.

"That's right. It wasn't that we didn't believe or were not that denomination, but because Dominic was the pastor. He tells us to believe in Jesus and steals innocence from our boys." Jan shook her head back and forth almost as if she had no control. Tears wet her cheeks faster than she could brush them away.

"Come here, Mom," Mike stands and pulls his mother to his chest and allows her to weep, holding her close. Only when the time was right, Mike asked one question that had been on his mind since he spoke with the Jones'. "Did Danny's mom ever mention anything to you about Dominic doing the same thing to her son?"

Jan lowered herself back into the chair and lifted the wine glass to her lips, draining the liquid. "She did. I told her that we haven't let our sons anywhere near my own brother for years and suggested that she not allow Danny to be near him, either.

"I did tell her she should look further into it if she suspected any wrongdoing. Unfortunately, Danny's family attended his church and were very involved with the congregational duties. And besides, things like that, trusted church leaders molesting young boys in their parish, just didn't happen in those days. Or, if it did, I never heard about it."

Jan stands to gaze out the French doors. "I blame myself for Sam's mental problems, even though I don't think it ever happened again. I truly believe that just one incident was enough for him to turn to drugs and alcohol as a way to cope.

"But maybe if I had taken it further, prosecuted Dominic, Sam would be a productive member of society, and maybe, just maybe your best friend would still be alive."

Steve walks into the dining room after overhearing part of the conversation. "What are you guys saying about my dad?"

"Nothing, sweetheart." Tear stains on Jan's cheeks tell Steve she's lying.

"Steve, that's not completely true." Mike nods to his mom and she closes her eyes. "I think you're old enough to hear about some adult problems. Some things your dad has been through are pretty ugly and very disturbing...Do you think you can handle knowing some family secrets?" Mike's lips purse and eyebrows raise while waiting for Steve to respond.

Steve pulls a seat away from the table and the chair legs scrape on the floor. Not sure yet how this adult conversation would go, Steve steals himself to prepare for the worst. He nods once, signaling that he is ready.

"We'll start with the obvious. Your dad is homeless because of his struggle with addiction. You know that, obviously, and unfortunately, it has affected all our lives—mostly yours. Some things happened in his childhood that your grandmother and I believe led to Sam making some really bad life choices.

"Beyond anyone's control, a very bad man abused your dad. We think Sam may have been molested when he was just a boy."

"You mean..." Steve gapes at his uncle in disbelief. "Like, someone...oh." Searching his grandma's face, Steve finds that she has the same expression as Mike. Head tilted, lips parted, eyes searching for understanding and offering empathy.

"Why would anyone want to do that to a little boy? You think that's why my dad is crazy?"

"Honey, your dad isn't crazy," Jan starts her rebuttal, then changes her mind. "Well, maybe he is a little crazy in a broad stroke of the word. His mind isn't the same as when you entered the world, especially from all the drugs he has taken.

Some people think substances blur the pain, but they only make things worse. Instead of finding someone to help him through a rough patch, your dad kept this to himself and now his mind isn't the same."

"How many years did he get away with this and how many boys did he abuse? Jesus, Mom, if I had known all this before, I would have beat his ass myself." Unable to sit still any longer, Mike rises and begins to pace.

"You mean my dad wasn't the only one? That's sick, dude." Steve's simplistic words articulate Mike's thoughts exactly.

In his mind, Mike remembers the days when Danny and he used to stop by the church once a week after class; it was a short drive from the high school to The Holy Cross. Mike never told his mom because he was not allowed to be anywhere near his uncle; he didn't know why but knew his dad would chap his ass if he found out.

Danny would visit with Dominic in his office while Mike sat in the sanctuary admiring the stained-glass windows decorated with Jesus, Mary, and the disciples. Twenty minutes later, Danny would emerge with red eyes and they would take a six-pack to the Falls.

He told Mike that his mom made him go to counseling because his grades had slipped. They did everything together and just because Mike's mom told him not to go near his uncle, didn't mean he couldn't follow his best friend to his weekly session at the church. Right?

Bile rose in Mike's throat forcing him to rush to the powder room to empty his stomach.

Once he returns to the dining room, Mike addresses his mother. "I have to see him. After knowing this, I have to look at him and process that he is the one common denominator for the most heinous crimes affecting those I love most. As a family, we need to be able to heal and put this behind us."

"WHAT, REBECCA?" Mike barks a little harsher than he meant.

"Michael, is that any way to address your wife? You need to check your attitude."

Just another jab, Mike ignores Rebecca's attempt

at controlling the situation. "I already told you I would be home on Sunday. Why are you calling me? Do you need the name of a moving company? I can call someone for you if you're having trouble..."

"That's enough," Rebecca interrupts. "Stop with this nonsense. I'm not going anywhere. You're coming home and we're going to work this out. We belong together. You need to take into consideration how entangled our lives are and how messy it would be to split."

"I'm not going to argue with you, Bec. You and all your shit need to be gone by Sunday. Period."

"How many times do I need to remind you that calling me that name only shows your redneck roots. Now, you listen to me..."

"No, God damn it," Mike interrupts. "You listen to me. We're over. Period. Get out of my house. Fucking leave and don't call me again." With a touch of his finger, the phone disconnects, and Rebecca's high-pitched voice is cut off.

Footsteps above Mike's head signal that Steve is pacing and Mike nods in understanding; he had been pacing, too. Unable to relax, especially after the conversation with Rebecca, Mike leans forward and puts his elbows on his knees.

He must be thinking, processing. Poor guy. I can't begin to comprehend how devastating this must be for a thirteen-year-old boy. Today sucks. Happy New Year, right?

Mike's hand rubs the scruff on his face and

decides it's time to shave. After all, Lisa said his beard tickled her nose.

After the stress of the day's events, determination propels Mike to reach out for help. The one person he trusts is 1,500 miles away but can easily be reached over the phone.

"Saul, hey. Do you have a couple minutes?"

"Mike, it's great to hear your voice. Of course, I have time for you. How is Tennessee?"

Briefly reviewing the day's events, Mike conveys the desperation not only with his voice but his words. Saul listens with minimal questions, only asking for enough information to understand how much his friend needs his support.

Chapter 13
JANUARY 2, 2015

Saul steps off the chartered jet at Crossville Memorial and instantly second-guesses his decision to spend time in Tennessee in January. He doesn't own any clothes which would be appropriate for temperatures under 70 degrees. When it's less than 60 degrees in LA, he stays inside.

"Holy shit it's cold!" Saul mutters as Coach closes the door to the Lincoln. "Why do people even live here?"

"It's not so bad. High today is supposed to be 43. First time to Tennessee? Where you from, friend?" Coach asks, unaware that Saul is Mike's friend.

"Los Angeles. Yes, first time; born and raised in California. I'm here visiting a friend. Guess I should have checked out the weather before scheduling a trip. Lesson learned." Saul searches for a way to increase the temperature in the backseat. As if the driver can read his mind, warm air begins to blow from the vents.

Coach smirks when Saul sighs and leans back in the seat. He can read most people and finds a way to give them exactly what they need. It's the little things that make such a big difference. "L.A., huh? Funny, I usually only see y'all a couple times a year, but you're the second person from L.A. that I've picked up this week. Where to?"

JAN ANSWERS the door in an apron that covers a baby blue blouse and slacks. A shivering medium-build man with thinning dark hair and glasses perched on the end of his nose stands on her front stoop and asks for Mike Allen.

Confused, Jan repeats the name of her son's California persona loud enough for Mike to overhear.

"Mom? Who is that at the door?" Footsteps on the tile proceed Mike into view. "Saul? Oh, my God. What are you doing here? Forget it, come in; it's practically freezing out there."

"Hi, Mike. You failed to mention that you have a younger sister," Saul winks at Jan and she waves away the compliment with her hand before turning toward the kitchen. "How are you, Mike? Surprise!"

"Saul, you are the best. Welcome, come in, come

in. You're just in time for dinner." Mike leads his friend into the kitchen and indicates he should sit at the bar, next to Steve. Glasses clink on the countertop and Mike asks what his friend would like to drink. A soda sits in front of Steve and Jan has already poured herself a glass of wine.

"I would love a glass of red, Mike. Thanks."

"Mom, Steve, this is my friend from L.A., Saul Goldman. Apparently, he got the hint that I could use a friend and chartered a jet to Oak Ridge. It's great to see you, my friend." With a nod toward Steve, Mike continues. "Saul, this is my nephew, Steve, and you have met my mother, Jan."

"A pleasure to meet you both! I have heard so much about you. I am so excited to see the little town that Mike describes with such passion and love." Jan winks over her shoulder and Steve offers a quiet "Hello."

"I hope you haven't made any hotel arrangements, Saul because you will stay in my guest room for as long as you need." Steam rises from the boiling pot of pasta and Jan points at Saul with a wooden spoon. He understands that no is not an option.

"Thank you, very much, Mrs. Allen. I appreciate that."

"Please, call me Jan," she requests of Saul. "What's with this Allen business?" Jan squints at her son.

"Oh, yeah. Did I not tell you that I changed my last name to Allen?"

Jan shakes her head and purses her lips.

Saul's eyes widen as he looks back and forth from Mike to Jan.

Mike explains, "Um, Higgenbottom is too hard to spell?"

A laugh escapes his mother's throat and she turns back to the stove. "Sure, Mike."

ROSIE CLEARS the table and Saul leans back in his chair. The aroma of garlic lingers. "Jan, dinner was spectacular. You are an incredible cook. Thank you again for having me."

Pink flushes Jan's cheeks and she's unsure if it is from the compliment or the glass of wine. "My pleasure, dear. How long do you plan to stay?"

"My wife went on a trip to Italy with a girlfriend, so there is no time limit," Saul says, "As long as I'm not an inconvenience, of course," he rushes to add.

"Mike just returned from Paris yesterday. Tell Saul about your trip with Lisa, sweetie."

"Lisa?" Saul's Left eyebrow raises as a sly grin reaches his lips. "Yes, please do tell."

"I've told you about Lisa. Well, she's always wanted to go to Paris, so I took her for New Year's Eve. I arranged a cooking lesson with her favorite chef, Jacques Devereaux, then he played tour guide for the rest of the day. You remember Jacques?"

Saul nods.

"He was fantastic; I always thought he would be the ideal person to accompany someone through the city. His knowledge of Parisian history is spot-on and he made Lisa feel like a princess."

Mike tells Saul about Lisa's top ten list, then adds, "I can't wait to take her back when we have more time. You and Lisette should join us. Seeing Saul's smile, Mike furrows his brows. "What?"

"Why, Mr. Higgenbottom, I don't believe I've ever seen your eyes sparkle when speaking of spending time with a young lady. Seems like this trip home was a very wise decision."

Mike laughs.

Ice cubes clink as Steve drains his soda and Mike changes gears. "What do you think, nephew of mine? Need a ride to Chase's house? Saul and I are going to visit Pops."

"Sure, Uncle Mike." Steve races up the steps to grab the necessities.

MOST OF ALLEN'S paintings resemble his late wife, Anna, a few are picturesque landscapes of local areas, and some, like his current work in progress, turn darker when he needs to chase the demons away.

Short strokes and strategically placed dabs lay brown paint over the hunter-green canvas as the aging man concentrates on the developing picture from a stool facing an easel.

Three brown figures lay on the ground in a forest with severe mountains that jut into the sky in the distance. Two of them are missing appendages; red paint accents the edges of limbs. One of the bodies is in multiple pieces, an expression of fear forever trapped on his face.

Once the staff psychologists determined that Allen suffered from PTSD, he tried to figure out the best form of therapeutic practice. Through trial and error, Allen and his psychologist found that painting helped soothe his anxiety, a discovery that surprised them both.

Mike clears his throat from the doorway, not wanting to startle his grandfather, and Allen turns to welcome his grandson and friend. "Pops, this is Saul. He's here visiting from California. Thought I would bring him by to say hi."

With a nod and glancing at each of his hands, Allen greets Saul. "I'd shake your hand, son, but painting is messy. Glad to meet you, Saul. Mike, you look like a regular person with a clean-shaven face. Grab a couple of those chairs and stay for a while."

"Thanks, Pops," Mike chuckles as he unfolds plastic chairs for Saul and himself. "You have such a talent for painting; where does this scene take place?" Mike surveys the canvas with knitted eyebrows. Saul tilts his head, already knowing what Allen will tell them as his eyes glaze over.

"They told me not to wear my uniform here in the states. People were against the war, so they were against us soldiers. Those of us who chose to sign up for duty may very well have given our lives for strangers and coming back to such ungrateful folks still burns my ass to this day. We fought a losing war on a foreign shore to find our country didn't want us back."

Allen drops the paintbrush into a cup of water, his eyes follow the motion of his hands as he wipes them on a towel. Mike catches his grandfather's gaze and Pops regains his focus.

"Unless you lived it, trust me when I say you have no idea what it was like. I had never in my wildest dreams expected to be soaked to the bone, carrying packs that weighed almost as much as I did, and walking for miles and miles and miles. Some of my men got jungle rot from walking through the swamps.

"We were terrified all the time. All of us. Never knowing when some guerrilla would start shooting, or who was next to be murdered; Billy, Donnie, and John lost their lives on my watch. Everyone said it wasn't my fault, but I blamed myself anyway.

"Every twig snapping under our feet would get us jumpy. Even if you were the biggest badass in your town before you went to 'Nam, you were scared shit-less while you were there.

"No one knew why we were even in 'Nam. We all had so many questions and not one of our superiors would give a straight answer. I prayed every day that my Anna would still love me after she found out what kind of man I had become. Painting lessens the effect of the flashbacks. Some nights I can sleep. A little.

"So many of us didn't have a choice; the draft took boys away from their family and friends. Took them away from the only life they ever knew or ever wanted to know. Didn't matter to some folks.

"You have probably heard stories about the things that happened when we went out in public, we were so humiliated." Allen turns to look out the window. "They spit on us; they threw rocks at us; they even vandalized our property. I came out of work one day to find big black spray-painted letters spelling out the words 'Baby Killer' on my car. How was I supposed to park in front of my home?"

Mike has always wanted to know more about Pop's time in the service. Now that his tongue is rolling, Mike wants him to continue, to know more about one of the men he's closest to in life.

"You're right," he confirms to his grandfather. "I have heard horror stories but had no idea that you had to face such dishonor. I'm so sorry." Hoping a simple question would keep him talking, he asks how long Pops served in the Army.

"I enlisted in '59 and served until '63. There was no future for me in Oakdale and I had a young family to support. Debt was piling up higher than I could reach and the service seemed like the best way to provide for my wife and kids.

"Your mom was only two, so I figured she wouldn't miss me. I was right; she didn't even recognize me when I came back home. Took her over a month to trust me enough to crawl on my lap, so I could hold her.

"Dominic was worse; he was five when I enlisted and eight when I got home. He acted out from the minute he saw my face, like he knew all the sins I committed in 'Nam. Like he couldn't stand to look at me. Got in all kinds of trouble, that kid. After a while, he stopped talking to me altogether." Pop's voice is shaky.

"It must have been so hard on all of the families trying to support their men." Saul's voice adds much-needed tranquility. "I can't imagine getting to know this lifestyle again and entering back into society."

"You're right. It was hard to fit in again, but I think it was harder for your grandma to get used to the new me. When I enlisted, I was pretty quiet and kind of shy. The service brought out the worst in me; by the time I came back, I cursed like a sailor and was loud and always looking for a fight. She said once that I wasn't the same man she married. She wasn't wrong.

"I started drinking pretty hard right after I got back; there was nothing better than the second my fingers wrapped around a frosty beer bottle on a hot summer day. It was a really difficult time for so many of us.

"Sometimes the smallest thing would trigger a flashback. A car door slamming, Dominic dropping a toy on the floor. God forbid you take your kids to a Fourth of July celebration. Jesus, that first time I thought I was back in the jungle I dropped to the ground and reached for an imaginary gun. Scared the shit out of your grandma. They didn't have a word for it then."

Curious, Saul asks, "How were you able to cope?"

"I tried really hard to just ignore it, but after a while, only liquor would quiet the noise. After the liquor wasn't enough, a couple old buddies introduced me to cocaine; with that came women.

"Hell, there was one girl who swears she gave birth to my son. I never got a chance to meet him because she moved to Virginia and cleaned up her life. Plus, I was still married. All I know is that she named him Eugene after her own Grandfather.

"I'm not proud of the time I spent in 'Nam and I'm sure as hell not proud of the man that came back from the war. Your grandma had an idea of what was happening, so she followed me one night and saw me with her. When she confronted me, I denied everything and walked out the door. When I came home drunk, she was gone.

"I would do just about anything to forget about my days in 'Nam. Nothing helped, really. I even tried to end it all, once. The way I see it, their bullets took my best friend in Saigon; our lawyers took my wife and kids, no regrets."

With pursed lips, Mike nods. "I'm really sorry, Pops."

"I made amends with your grandma after I got better. Every day I ask God to forgive me for what I've done there, 'cause I never meant the things I did."

"HEY, Mike. I need to tell you something," As Saul opens the passenger door, he hesitates.

"Okay," Mike drags out the word and tilts his head.

"I didn't know for sure that Rebecca was having an affair, but I'm not surprised."

"What do you mean by that?" Mike's eyebrows lift.

"I didn't want to tell you this over the phone, so I'm glad I had this opportunity to visit." Saul takes a deep breath before confessing. "Two years ago, at the Laminsol party, Rebecca came on to me and tried to kiss me. We were alone on the roof of the Spire 73 and she...touched me...before she propositioned me.

"I can't remember the exact words, but she said

something like 'I've seen you fuck me with your eyes, wanna use this instead?' as she squeezed me. I was absolutely stunned and of course, I declined. I never found the right time to tell you. Until now."

A sigh and pursed lips proceed Mike's understanding nod. "That explains a lot, actually. She cringes at the sound of your name."

Saul laughs at the unexpected reply from his friend. Relieved, he slaps Mike on the shoulder before easing into the passenger side of the BMW.

Mike turns the ignition as he speaks. "You know, I only ever told Rebecca that I loved her when she made me say it or if I wanted something from her. I never really did have strong feelings for her. Not like Lisa. Lisa is the real deal."

Chapter 14
JANUARY 3, 2015

Curves through the Appalachian foothill towns of Glenmary, Elgin, and Robbins remind Mike of trips to Lexington in the 90s to see Lisa's favorite artists, Britney and Justin. Throughout the years they dated, they must have seen *NSYNC a dozen times. Mike has a feeling that this trip isn't going to be nearly as enjoyable.

Saul took it upon himself to make an appointment to visit Dominic at McCreary Federal Prison located just across the Kentucky border. Mike is pleasantly surprised to discover that he is content with a friend taking control. "Thank you for handling the details of this visit; you must know me better than I know myself."

"That's my job; I have read between the lines for so many years, it comes naturally, now. A blessing and a curse. For friends, I consider it a contribution." Saul flashes a quick smile to Mike.

"When you called, you mentioned that your family needs to heal and asked if I could help on a personal level. Confronting the individual at the center of the turmoil is essential to the healing process. I know which steps to take to help you achieve success as quickly as possible.

"Please understand that this could get ugly. For you both. This conversation will explore things that Dominic doesn't want to admit and it may open doors to information you don't know exists. Are you ready for that?"

"I am ready," Mike confirms with a nod. "It's time to put this to bed. By the way, how did you know where my uncle is incarcerated?"

"Your uncle's conviction is a public record, so anyone can access the details. Before we get there, I would like to talk about Danny. That's the reason you came home and why I offered to drive."

Saul turns to Mike and asks him to take a couple deep breaths and clear his mind. "Find one object to concentrate on and focus on that object, alone. Tell me when you know what that is."

Dotted lines of US-27 help Mike relax into a trance-like state and he informs Saul of his decision to focus on those lines.

"Watch each of the lines disappear under the bumper. With each line gone, you feel the tension ease from your shoulders. I want you to take one more deep breath before you tell me about Danny. First, describe every detail you can remember from the day you two met."

After Mike exhales the last bit of tension, he begins the exercise.

LEATHER CUFFS secure Dominic McKay's thin wrists to the hospital bed. His sunken cheeks, wide eyes, and bald head render the pastor unrecognizable to Mike. At the prime of his success, Dominic had luscious locks and a solid frame; most of the women in the congregation found him irresistible.

"Mr. McKay is quite frail, so please take care to not say anything to upset him," a nurse enters the room and pushes a few buttons on the monitors before she leaves. The scent of latex follows her.

Mike glances at Saul, huffs, and rolls his eyes as he steps toward the bed. *I'll be goddamned if I keep my words courteous for this excuse for a human being.*

"Mike? Is that you? They told me you were coming today, but I thought maybe it was a dream." Dominic's weak smile does not reach his eyes. "Some days I am blessed to have enough pain medication to allow hallucinations."

Mike's disgust is evident to Saul and the guard who silently observes from the far corner of the room. Without patience for pleasantries, Mike confronts his uncle. "You know, when I was little, I thought all sins would be forgiven simply because you believed in God. It wasn't until I was older that I understood that God is willing to forgive our sins as long as we confess and ask for forgiveness."

"Where are you going with this, son?" Dominic turns his head to get a good look at his nephew.

"Don't call me son. You don't have the right to address me as family. After what you've done to my brother and best friend, you deserve every bit of what you've received in this prison. Including the cancer that's eating away at you little by little."

Dominic's eyebrows knit and he shakes his head. Saul observes his friend from a distance and keeps a careful watch on Mike's emotions.

"I know what you did to Sam—my brother is homeless because he couldn't chase away his demons with alcohol alone. My mom told me about the night my dad beat your ass, but that obviously didn't stop you from preying on Danny Jones.

"My best friend is dead because of you, took his own life because the memory of what you did to him was too much to bear. How many others were there, Dominic? How many other lives did you ruin?"

"What are you talking about? I never hurt anyone. I may have kept a lover and embezzled from the church to give him everything he wanted, but that doesn't mean I hurt anyone. I'm doing my time for my crime." Exhaustion causes the prisoner to close his eyes as his breathing quickens. Beeps come from the machines tied to him and a nurse enters the room.

"You'll have to leave, now. Mr. McKay has had enough. He needs to rest." The nurse points to the door and the guard disguises a chuckle with an exaggerated cough.

"It's okay, Mike is my nephew and it's been years since we spoke. I want him to stay." Dominic uses his charm on the nurse and she shrugs before walking out the door.

"You're right, Mike." Dominic focuses on Mike's face. "I have to confess to be forgiven; I need to get this off my chest, once and for all." Exaggerated deep breaths extend the time between Dominic's words. "I never told anyone who the man was that I went to prison for. If I had given his name, my sentence would have been shorter.

"Your friend, Daniel, and I had a relationship for many years. I stole money from the hands of my parishioners to keep him happy. We were in love."

Not believing his ears, but aware that he must listen to Dominic, Mike forces himself to stay calm. Those four words are an outright lie. Aren't they?

If they were in love, Danny would have told me. Wouldn't he? We were brothers and shared everything. He would have never had a serious girlfriend. Would he? Oh, Jesus. What don't I know? Was Danny gay and ashamed to say anything? I would have been okay with it, wouldn't I? I don't know what to believe anymore. God help me.

"You have no idea how hard it is for me to be in here, a preacher in prison. I've been beaten bloody, stabbed with a shank, strangled, and held down by grown men while each of them raped me. Repeatedly."

"No. No, no, no. You are not the victim here. You are a fucking murderer as far as I'm concerned. You killed my best friend. You're a fucking pedophile that sought out little boys. You're barely human." Heat rises from Mike's neck to his cheeks as he glares at his uncle.

Saul steps forward, "This isn't getting us anywhere, Mike. We need to be productive."

Mike raises his hand to signal that he will remain calm before starting to pace.

With a nod from Mike, Dominic continues. "I am not a murderer. I loved Daniel. I wanted to spend my life with him. Yes, I groomed him and that was wrong, but he was the only one. I never touched your brother, I swear."

"Then who did? You dropped him off one night and he told my mom about the game you played with him. That you hurt him. I don't believe a word you're saying."

"Mike, I...I know this doesn't make it sound any better, but my stepdad started to molest me when I was just a boy and he made me believe we were meant to be together forever. I wanted to be with him, but when my mother found out four years later, she forced him to leave. My heart was broken until I found Daniel." Dominic closes his eyes and a smirk forms on his lips as he remembers his younger days.

"He resisted until I bought him presents; even after I bought him a Camaro, he couldn't admit that he loved me. I gave him cash and paid his bills. I guess you could say that I forced him into the relationship, forced him to do things he didn't want to do, and for that I am sorry. But I had to have him.

"I tried to apologize to him by sending a photo of us at my cabin near Knoxville as a way to make amends. We were so happy when we were alone. In the woods, no one could see the way he looked at me."

"You're either lying or delusional," Mike interrupts. "Either way, the suicide note that Danny wrote his parents tells a totally different story. He's not here to defend himself, so I will take on that battle. The way he tells it, he didn't have a choice; you threatened to make his life hell if he didn't do what you wanted.

"You bought him things that he could never afford on his own and threatened to tell everyone that he was gay. Who cares if he was, the point is that you used your influence in the community to make him think he was alone, that no one would believe him if he told the truth.

"He said you called him Sam once, so I know

you're lying about not touching my brother." Mike intentionally uses harsh words to upset his uncle. He's furious and wants to inflict pain.

"Danny was finally starting to heal when he received the photo from you; he said it was a threat and believed that his life was over. Do you know what you did to his family? His mother still cries every day. His dad is disturbed and holds hatred in his heart.

"If you're looking for forgiveness, you won't get it from me. My brother abandoned his son because he won't allow himself to have a meaningful life. Because of you. My mother, your own sister, is embarrassed to call you her brother. You have single-handedly ruined three families with your sick ways.

"I wish you were well," Mike's voice softens as he steps toward the bed. Light and a touch of hope return to Dominic's eyes. "I honestly do, but not for the reason you think. I wish you were well enough to beat the living shit out of. I wish I could finish what my dad started all those years ago."

Warm hands grip the cool metal of the hospital bed, next to the restraint. Mike leans closer to Dominic, his voice is barely audible. "He should have kept hitting you, over and over and over, until your lifeless body hit the ground."

Mike catches a glimpse of the guard rising off his stool and takes a step back. "Nothing you say can make what you did to my best friend acceptable. You may call yourself my uncle, but you're dead to me. You're a sick fuck and I hope you rot in hell."

Dominic's eyes close as the color leaves his face. Saul follows Mike out of the room.

Mike hesitates outside the prison doors, leans over the railing, and pukes in the bushes. Once his stomach stops retching, he slides down the cold brick wall and crouches on the sidewalk. With his head between his hands, uncontrollable gasps escape as Mike sobs for his dead best friend.

Saul's arm wraps around Mike's shoulders as they shake. His comforting grip conveys the strength and compassion needed for his friend to gather himself and stand.

Once they reach the BMW Saul feels it's the right time to inform Mike that he knows more about Dominic than he admitted. "A couple of my contacts were able to get ahold of more information than is available to the public. I wasn't sure how much you knew, so I didn't discuss details before we arrived because your reaction needed to be genuine.

"Dominic admitted to molesting five boys, Danny being the last. His file has testimony from those boys to back that story. Your anger is expected and acceptable; now we can work to heal you and your family."

Reverend Paul Savatgy of Oak Ridge Presbyterian Church offers the Call to Worship as distinct organ music plays in the background. Being Jewish, Saul considered staying at the house, but out of curiosity, he decides to attend the Sunday service with Mike's family. He keeps an open mind during the first portion of the service and prepares to focus on the teaching point of the Sermon.

After the children's message concludes, Lisa follows fifteen youngsters down the center aisle, and Mike catches her eye. A wave of his hand signals an offer to join his family. Jan and Steve sit at the far end of the pew and Saul stands to let Lisa sit next to Mike.

Lisa rests her hand on Mike's knee, leans close, and whispers "I love this face." Rose scented perfume brings a smirk to Mike's lips as he kisses her on the cheek. Visions of intimate moments with Lisa in high school flood his memory and Mike tries to wipe them away—this is church, after all. Jan winks at the couple and extends a wave and a warm smile.

Static from the Reverend's microphone is quickly remedied and he addresses his congregation. "Yesterday afternoon, I was walking through the mall with my wife and daughter. We searched every store that had shoes for the perfect basketball sneakers for Karissa.

"She continued to get frustrated with every pair that wasn't quite the right color, just didn't fit right, or weren't in style. After she snapped at her mom one time too many, Leah sat her down and had a heart-to-heart about how to treat people when you're frustrated.

"Karissa apologized and Leah said that she forgave her. How many times in the past year have I heard that phrase: 'I forgive you'? Their heart-to-heart reminded me how easily forgiveness can come and also how difficult it can be to forgive. Some situations require so much work that we often give up and give in to anger. Today, I will be talking about Forgiveness.

"Forgiveness is a choice we make. It is a decision of our will, motivated by obedience to God and his command to forgive. The Bible instructs us to forgive as the Lord forgave us. There are many instances in the Bible that teach us to forgive, how to forgive, and when to forgive.

"*'Bear with each other and forgive whatever grievances you may have against one another. Forgive as the Lord forgave you. (Colossians 3:13)'*

"Because forgiveness goes against our nature, we must forgive by faith, whether we feel like it or not. We must trust God to do the work in us that needs to be done so that our forgiveness will be complete. Our faith brings us confidence in God's promise to help us forgive and shows that we trust in his character.

"*'Faith shows the reality of what we hope for; it is the evidence of things we cannot see. (Hebrews 11:1)'*

"But you may ask, how will I know if I have truly forgiven? We will know the work of forgiveness is complete when we experience the freedom that comes as a result. We are the ones who suffer most when we choose not to forgive.

"When we do forgive, the Lord sets our hearts free from the anger, bitterness, resentment, and hurt that previously imprisoned us. Most of the time, forgiveness is a slow process.

"*'Then Peter came to Jesus and asked, "Lord, how many times shall I forgive my brother or sister who sins against me? Up to seven times?" Jesus answered, "I tell you, not seven times, but seventy-seven times. (Matthew 18:21-22)'*

"Jesus was saying, keep on forgiving until you experience the freedom of forgiveness. Forgiveness may require a lifetime of forgiving, but it is important to the Lord. We must continue forgiving until the matter is settled in our hearts.

"Is it okay to feel anger and want justice for the person we need to forgive? We can trust God to judge that person's life and then we no longer have to carry the anger. Although it is normal for us to feel anger toward sin and injustice, it is not our job to judge the other person in their sin.

"'*Do not judge, and you will not be judged. Do not condemn, and you will not be condemned. Forgive, and you will be forgiven. (Luke 6:37)*'

The Reverend's voice fades in Mike's mind and he is drawn to gaze at the balcony at the front of the church. The upper level is empty, but the image of Danny sits in the front row, elbows on knees with his head in his hands.

A peaceful wave overcomes Mike and he sends his best friend a telepathic message that it's okay, he is forgiven for his sins. *All the confusion and negative energy can be put behind us, now, Danny. Moving forward, your memory will be a blessing and a celebration. I can see you up there, thank you for showing yourself to me.*

I can understand how places like this may not be the most comfortable for you. Not that it matters now, but I get it. After today's reminder, I just may be able to forgive my uncle. If not completely, at least maybe I can let go of some of the anger.

I needed to hear this message today, and I think you did too. You can forgive yourself, now, my friend.

Reverend Paul's voice is audible once again and peace seeps into Mike's soul. "Why must we forgive? The best reason to forgive is simple: Jesus commanded us to forgive. We learn from scripture in context to forgiveness that if we don't forgive, neither will we be forgiven.

"'*For if you forgive men when they sin against you, your heavenly Father will also forgive you. But if you do not forgive men their sins, your Father will not forgive your sins. (Matthew 6:14-16)*'

"In summary, we forgive out of obedience to the Lord. It is a choice, a decision we make. However, as we do our part 'forgiving,' we discover the command to forgive is in place for our own good, and we receive the reward of our forgiveness, which is spiritual freedom."

AFTER THE SERVICE parishioners gather in the community room; coffee, tea, cookies, and cake cover tables along one wall. Lisa holds Mike's hand as they wait for Jan and Steve to wade through the line.

"Well, what did you think?" Mike asks Saul, knowing his friend will provide honest feedback.

"The message of forgiveness was exceptional. Even though I don't have the same beliefs of who said what to whom, I can admit that the words were very helpful. Forgiveness can be an incredible stress-reliever and give those forgiving a sense of peace. Thank you for inviting me to join you, today. It has been a pleasure."

Although Reverend Paul makes it a point to welcome every visitor each Sunday, he noticed Saul's kippah as he sat in the congregation and set a mental reminder to find him immediately after the service. "Welcome. I am Reverend Paul Savatgy. I am so pleased to meet you." An outstretched hand invites Saul to respond.

"Saul Goldman. The pleasure is all mine. What a wonderful sermon. I was just telling my friend, Mike, that it was a pleasure to hear you speak."

Jan settles next to her son and nods to Reverend Paul. With an understanding smile, he continues.

"Thank you for the compliment. Everyday life has a way of showing us how important messages can be discovered, formed into a learning experience, and shared with those we love. I am always thrilled to have friends from other religions visit our little community. Please, let me know if you need anything. Jan here knows how to get in touch with me."

SUN RADIATES behind Lisa as she stands in her driveway waiting for Mike to park the BMW behind her Toyota. Never one to wear high-heels, black pumps complete the ensemble of a simple hunter green dress and black wool coat.

She looks like an angel. I am so blessed.

Following her through the side door, Mike removes his coat and hangs it on a peg next to Lisa's. "You look fantastic, Lisa. That dress is beautiful and I have always loved when you pull your hair back."

A hearty laugh escapes before Mike kisses her cheek. "Oh, honey, don't blush. I've missed you these past couple of days. Even though we sent texts here and there, I missed your eyes. And the most, your smile."

Mike cups Lisa's cheek, his hand is warm as he presses his lips against hers. Lisa inhales deeply as she responds to his kiss. A smile forms on Mike's lips before he parts hers. The couple finds themselves in an intense embrace, which neither wants to stop.

Mike wraps one arm around Lisa's waist and pulls her closer, a mirror to their dance in Paris. Refusing to break the kiss, he leads her to the living room and they sit on the couch.

"I've missed you, too, Mike. Not just these past few days, but years. Can you tell?" Lisa's forehead rests against Mike's as they both struggle to catch their breath. Opening her eyes to gaze into Mike's, she continues, "the passion I felt for you all those years ago, has resurfaced. I would love to take you to my bedroom and spend hours showing you how I feel, but it's obviously not the right time."

"Damn it," Mike jokes and winks. "I have so much to tell you, but I'm afraid it will ruin the mood."

"We'll get this mood back, Mike. Don't you worry about that." A deep kiss later, Lisa rises and informs her guest that she will return in a couple of minutes.

Jeans and a form-fitting sweater show off Lisa's figure as she settles on the couch. Mike smiles in response and curses himself for not following her into her bedroom. He reminds himself that there will be time for passion later.

"You said you have so much to tell me." Lisa's soft tone relaxes Mike. "I appreciate that we keep in contact through text, but there's only so much you can convey without hearing each other's voice. I slept most of the day New Year's Day—someone wore me out in Paris," Lisa steals another kiss, "and Saul came to visit you; how nice. He's a good friend."

"The best. Almost," Mike frowns at the thought of someone replacing Danny. "On the way to Paris, I almost told you all this, but I didn't want to ruin the perfect day I had planned. On the way home, I was on such a high that I didn't want to ever come down."

Lisa's hand is soft under his. "I understand."

"Saul and I went to Kentucky to visit my Uncle Dominic and I will tell you all about that in a minute. I want to fill you in on some other things, first, so you can grasp the entire picture and appreciate why today's sermon of forgiveness meant so much to me.

"You know all about Steve and Sam. Probably more than I do, but you don't know everything about Danny. I met with his parents last Saturday. They shared with me the letter that he wrote the day he ended his life."

Will it ever get easier to say that phrase?

"You know that my Uncle Dominic is in prison for embezzling from his church. His story was that he had 'kept' a man and he refused to name that person for a reduced sentence." Pausing, Mike searches Lisa's eyes. She hasn't yet guessed the name of the 'kept' man.

"Danny was Uncle Dominic's 'friend'."

"What? I'm sorry, Mike. That doesn't make sense. Did you say, Danny? Your Danny? Our Danny?"

Tears fall from Lisa's eyes as her head tilts and eyebrows knit. Mike's heart sinks to his stomach at the realization that Lisa understands the magnitude of the situation.

Chapter 16
JANUARY 5, 2015

After Mike informs his dad of the plan, Ronnie offers to loan him a truck off the used car lot. If Mike and Saul drive past Sam's camp at a slow pace, the 2005 F-150 could resemble a volunteer's vehicle.

Last week when Mike drove by, he tried not to stare as each man watched the Buick with suspicion. His mom's car is out of place in this area but not nearly as much as the BMW would be.

Shadows conceal the frown and pinched eyebrows that plague Mike's face. "It's heartbreaking to see all these people living on the streets. My God, their bodies are in an open grave. What have these poor men and women suffered in their lives? What put them here?

"A mile away live the rich folks, without a care in

the world, just living it up. Do they even realize that almost in their own backyard, poor men and women eat from hand to mouth while they drink from a golden cup? It just makes me wonder why so many lose and so few win."

Tension laced with anxiety fills the cab of the truck. Saul senses the emotions and wonders aloud about the next step: "What are you going to do if you find him, Mike? When you find him."

"Jesus, I haven't even thought of that." The truck slows to a crawl on the cold dark street. As Mike studies the seriousness on Saul's face, he pulls over to the curb and throws the gear shifter into Park. A street light flickers above as if the electricity doesn't quite reach the top of the pole.

White knuckles begin to glow in the dark as Mike's grip intensifies on the steering wheel. A deep breath and long exhale help release the pressure in his shoulders. A little.

"I always looked up to my big brother. I used to follow him around like a puppy dog. If he went to his room to get away from my mom and dad arguing, I followed. If he went to the barn after dinner to play with the kittens, I was right on his heels. When he tinkered on the motorcycle, I mimicked his motions on the four-wheeler. We did everything together."

Memories flood back and Mike shares them with Saul. "After he started hanging around some older shady kids at school, he kept me on the outskirts, pushed me away.

"I often have to stop myself from thinking about how he used to be because of all the shit he has put my mom through. Dumping Stevie on her was bad enough, but never coming to see him and not helping with the smallest things has made me lose all respect for Sam.

"No birthday or Christmas presents, no help with homework, no new shoes, not even watching a movie together. I don't get how someone can be like that; just leave your son? Cut all ties?"

Saul listens intently and without interruption until Mike pauses. "You know, Mike. I have heard stories like this before. Some of my clients have homeless children or siblings, even parents.

"It's often the result of a mental imbalance that some people can't explain, and others can't under-stand. You haven't ever been in his situation, so it's difficult for you to grasp how he feels or why he acts the way he does.

"Drugs have played a huge role in the way Sam has decided to live his life. Most of the time, it's the drugs that lead the way, not your brother. Unless you've experienced the mental break that these folks have lived through, you can't understand. I'm trained in this type of thing and I'll be damned if I under-stand fully."

"After he lost his job," Mike continues, "Sam started bouncing from friend to friend until they either got arrested or kicked him out. From what I understand, he had to steal to contribute to the bills, so he started dealing cocaine.

"Eventually, he got arrested and sentenced to six months for past drug warrants; at least he got to spend the summer in air conditioning." Mike's attempt at seeing the silver lining falls short.

Vibration from Mike's phone sitting on the dash startles the men. Mike answers without looking at the screen.

"Michael? Where are you? Are you okay?" The shrill words from Rebecca's voice cause Mike to shudder. "My God, I've been worried sick. You said you would be home yesterday. What the fuck do you expect me to do when I worry so much about you?

"I had a dream that you were dead and when I woke up, your place in bed was empty. Are you there, Mike? Mike?"

"You were supposed to be out of my house yesterday, Bec. You know what? I don't have time for this. I'm in the middle of something way more important than talking to you. If you're not out by tomorrow, I'm calling the police to have you removed." With a touch of his finger, the phone disconnects.

Mike shakes his head as he glances at Saul and pulls away from the curb.

ON A HALF-ACRE LOT behind the local Home Depot, shopping carts full of previously discarded blankets, bags, and boxes surround multiple tents. One of the three known homeless tent communities in Oak Ridge, the population of this area fluctuates between twenty and thirty people on any given night.

Though the city allows the tent areas to exist, if it receives enough complaints, it will forcibly move the homeless population. They live with the constant worry of forced transience.

Several sets of dirty fingers hover above flames that rise out of an old metal fifty-five-gallon drum, absorbing the heat. One man wears a tight flannel shirt, the original pattern of red and white plaid has turned to a dingy brown and tan over the years. His thin arms are too long for the fabric to cover his pale wrists.

Sam Higgenbottom holds a bottle of Ten High whiskey in one hand and a cigarette in the other. He sways from right to left before spreading his feet into a steady stance. Strands of greasy hair, which was once blond, hang in the old, poor drunk's face, hiding half-closed eyes.

Three other men share the heat from the burn barrel and whiskey. And Joni. For the past three months these five people learned to depend on each other because, in their opinion, everyone else is just weird.

"Don't hog it all, Higgs, man. Pass that bitch." A gruff voice from across the fire forces Sam to focus through blurry vision.

Sam's crusty lips meet the bottle for one more swig before he shares it with his friends. Amber liquid drips into Sam's tangled beard and he tries to wipe it away with the back of his hand. Instead, it seeps into his beard, making it wet.

"The bottle or the bitch?" Sam doesn't laugh when he glances at Joni.

As Joni stumbles away from the burn barrel, she bumps the back of her calves against a frayed lawn chair that catches her when she falls. "Wha...?"

Sam backs away from the barrel, too, the alcohol warms his insides. His eyes heavy and skin warm from the fire, Sam drops into the broken golf chair next to the sole woman of the group. "Man, I love this chair. I was so lucky to find it on the golf course last summer...".

Sam's snores rise into the cold air before his friends have a chance to respond.

"Florida and Fairbanks or the Fire Station?" Joni mumbles to herself as she tries to decide where to start begging the next day. "The Fire Station isn't a bad place to set up; the firefighters are flamin' hot and they sometimes give me dollars instead of coins.

"Maybe the corner of Tyler and Administration. Fuck, I love that place. Fast Food all around and a park to get away if someone offers more than food. I'd give anyone a blow job for a fucking burger."

"OH, my God. I think that's him," Mike stops the truck and points to a burn barrel surrounded by thin bodies clothed in baggy layers. One of them sits in a chair, seemingly passed out. "My mom was right; behind the Home Depot, under a broken old billboard that used to read 'Jesus Saves'. Sam. Holy shit. What has become of you?" The cab of the truck absorbs his question as Mike pulls the handle to open the door.

"Wait, Mike." Saul reaches for his friend's arm. "Are you sure? Think about this for a minute,"

"That's Sam. I'm sure."

"Okay but hear me out. If you barge into this area, you could upset the entire society. People are here because they are comfortable living this way; we must tread lightly."

Mike thinks about this for a moment. "You're right. I didn't think about what it would do to everyone besides Sam if a stranger just shows up out of the blue demanding to speak with one of their own. They could think we want to disturb their way of living or that we're the police."

Mike considers his options as his gaze remains on the sleeping bum. "We could drive up and announce that we're here for Sam, but that might scare him away. We could act like we're one of them, but they wouldn't buy it. Do we act like a volunteer? What is the best move, here?"

Saul's thumb and forefinger rub his smooth chin as he forms the right words. "We go slow and calm. Hands visible, so they can see we're not going to hurt them. You must treat them with caution, sort of as a pack; they only trust each other. If we lie about why we're here, they will see through that, too.

"We go slow and calm, hands visible," Mike repeats and adds, "and ask for Sam. He'll know me; he'll know I'm here to help." He seeks support from his friend. "Right?"

"I sincerely hope so, Mike." Strong fingers grip Mike's shoulder before Saul nods. "Ready?"

SNAPS AND CRACKS echo from the fire as a broken pallet board is added to the barrel. Flames rise into the dark as Sam stands when he hears someone say his name.

"Man, I swear I was only talkin', I ain't sellin' no shit."

"Sam. Hey, man. It's me, Mike."

"I don't know no Mike," Sam searches the area around him and finds his friends ready to protect the

214

only items they own. Two of the other men hold some sort of weapon, a pallet board, and a flashlight.

"What the fuck do you want? Get the fuck out of here before someone gets hurt." Sores on Sam's hands and dirt under his fingernails are visible in the dark. The blade of the knife in his hand does not reflect the light of the fire.

Mike's stomach sinks as he wonders whose blood is on the knife held by his brother. He reminds himself to keep cool like Saul next to him. One arm reaches toward his friend, palm facing out. "Sam, I'm your brother, Mike. It's me. Remember? I came back from California to see you."

"My fucking brother died." Glassy eyes dart from Saul to Mike and back with no sense of recognition.

"No, Sam. It's me. Look at me, I'm here. It's Mike."

It can't end like this. We can't walk away letting him think I'm dead. I have to convince him that it's me. What happened when we were young that I know he could never forget? Damn it, man think!

"Sam, listen. Remember that day you, Danny, and I went fishing up at the old McTaggert place? That bear almost killed all three of us. He must have chased us clear to the river. I was so scared that I would never get a chance to drive your car. Remember?"

"Mike?" Squinted eyes examine his brother and Saul. "Danny?"

Surprised that he breaks through and confused from the second name his brother says, Mike's eyebrows raise and he glances at Saul who shakes his head.

"It will just confuse him if you give too much info. It's okay. Roll with it," Saul says.

"Yeah, man. Hey. How the hell are ya?" As soon as the words come out of his mouth, Mike shakes his head at the obviously ridiculous question.

"Mike!" Teeth rotted from years of using meth fill a smile that Mike is convinced has rarely been used in the past few years. Sam lunges at his brother with arms held out at his side. "Come here you moth-erfucker."

Body odor, whiskey, and stale cigarettes assault Mike's nostrils and he forces himself to stand in place. Backing away from the rank scents would certainly break the newfound fragile bond. Dirty hands grab each side of Mike's face as split lips crush his cheek. A shudder escapes that Mike is unable to control.

"Dude, you scared off my friends." Sam searches the area for the other men. "They had the fucking whiskey." Hoarse, slurred speech puts Mike on guard. "Here, sit," Sam says. The broken golf chair drags on the ground as he offers Mike a seat.

Turning to Saul, Sam apologizes, "Sorry, Danny. I only have one." Shoulders raise before Sam's thin frame sinks to the ground. He settles in an Indian-style position in front of Mike.

"Man, it's good to see you. I can hardly believe you're here. My brother...man." Soft words and a smile change the tone of the conversation. "Someone told me you died. Who would say that?"

"No, Sam. I'm right here. I don't know who would say such a thing." Mike shakes his head and pushes back thoughts of how different Sam is from the last time they were together. "What happened, man? Are you okay here? How can I help you?"

The scene is almost impossible to grasp; his idol is dead, replaced by a lumpy pile of skin and bones with the slight resemblance of his brother; his very first friend.

"I fall all the time. I have bruises on every part of my body. People steal my shit, so I keep a knife on me." His dirty blade is revealed for a second, then hidden. "I haven't had to use it yet. Unless you count when Joni tried to fuck me the day she got here. That was more of an accident, though. She reached for it, so it was her fault."

"We all share everything here. Once a week, we have McDonald's. Fridays. People on the road throw rocks at us all the time. I have bruises on every part of my body. They took my fucking whiskey," he rambles.

"Joni tried to fuck me when she got here. I almost had to kill her. She's a fucking freak but so are the guys. Is it Friday? I would love some fucking McDonald's. We all share everything, especially the weed." Cracked hands pat the pockets of the flannel. "Where's my fucking whiskey?"

Saul's calm reaction shows that he has been near people with severe problems in the past. He acts like he knows exactly what Sam is talking about; like he's not all over the place and repeating himself.

With it impossible to carry a direct conversation, Mike and Saul follow Sam's lead as long as they can. Confused and frustrated, they understand when it's time to leave. Mike tucks a business card with Jan's phone number written on the back into the breast pocket of Sam's flannel.

"Sam, when you're ready to see Steve and mom and be a part of our family again, I can help you. When you're ready to eat good meals and be warm every night, I can help you. I put mom's phone number in your pocket. When you decide you're ready, call me."

MIKE WALKS through the side door to his mom's gigantic house with tears running down his cheeks. Jan's smile disappears after she turns to greet him, unaware of where he has been. Mike's arms envelop her and hold her so tightly that her mom senses kick in. Every muscle in her body tightens in response.

"We found Sam, but it's not him anymore. My brother's gone."

Jan nods her understanding and embraces her son as her tears dampen the front of his shirt. She understands. She, too, has spent many nights grieving the loss of her oldest son.

Chapter 17
JANUARY 6, 2015

Mockingbirds fly to and from the bird feeder as Jan sits at the breakfast table, the phone still in her hand. Memories of her childhood fill her mind instead of the nature scene in front of her. Dominic pushing her on the swing, beating up the boy the pushed her down in fifth grade, and tripping up the steps at his high school graduation.

Growing up without a true father figure, Jan's brother had had her back in any situation and she loved him for it. A single tear slips down her cheek as she remembers the day she realized how evil Dominic had become. There had been something off about him for years, but she never dreamed that he had become a pedophile.

"Hey. Are you okay? Who was that on the phone?"

Jan startles at the sound of her son's voice.

Furrowed brows show the concern on Mike's face as he touches her arm from across the table. "Mom?"

"McCreary County. Dominic died last night. His last wish was to be cremated and buried in the cemetery at The Holy Cross Church, but they refused to take him. The prison asked if I had made any secondary plans." Jan searches the face of her son as tears form in her eyes.

"I told them no. I don't know what they will do with him and I don't really want to know." A deep breath exits her chest as she squints at her son. "I can't figure out how I should feel. Is it bad to be relieved?" Pink fingernails tap the tabletop as Jan ponders her emotions.

Saul fills a mug with coffee and joins them at the table. "Jan, it's okay to feel relief. When someone causes so much pain in one family, it's natural to not be sad when they pass." The sound of his voice eases the tension in Jan's shoulders allowing her to calm down.

"Some families believe that when someone is so sick and they keep clinging to life, they must be waiting for something specific to happen before they let go. In Dominic's case, it seems that he waited for the truth to be released," Saul tilts his head and smiles at Jan.

"The truth will set you free," Mike didn't realize he spoke out loud until Jan looked at him. "Mom, I'm sorry that your brother is gone, but hasn't he been gone for years?

"That's probably not what you need to hear and because I can't say anything nice, I'm not going to express my feelings about this in front of you. Not right now." Mike turns to leave and in a low, hard voice says, "Please excuse me."

SUNLIGHT BREAKS through the window and stretches across the bed in Mike's room. Warmth on his face brings a smile to his lips and tears to his eyes. Sandalwood and Cedar scents of Dolce & Gabbana fill the space next to Mike and he swears he sensed the mattress sink next to him. A hint of citrus and lavender confirms that Danny is nearby.

"It's over, man. He's finally gone. The psychotic piece of shit that ruined your life is now burning in hell.

"What I wouldn't give to have you in full-body form, so I can see your face, shake your hand, and wrap my arms around you. Instead, I sit alone in my room, so no one thinks I'm crazy talking to your spirit.

"No, I really don't care what anyone thinks, but you know my mom. She'd freak. Remember that time we brought the Ouija board home and tried to summon the spirit of the old man that owned the house before us? She swears after that night someone made the floors squeak when my dad was out late.

"Listen to me, talking to you like you're alive. God damn it, why did you think there was no other way? I don't want to be mad at you, but fuck, dude, couldn't I have helped? Wasn't there something I could have done to ease your pain? You know I would have killed the fucker for you...Oh, yeah... Then I would be the one in prison.

"Oh, Danny. Okay. What's done is done. You can rest, but please don't leave me again. I want you to be able to move on to a new soul, but I like knowing that you're here.

"That's selfish of me, isn't it? I can't keep you to myself just because I miss you like fucking crazy. Your smile, your laugh, your stupid phrases, the way your entire demeanor changed when a lady was around.

"So, this is it? Time to say goodbye? But not forever, right? Promise you'll come back to me in some form? A cardinal, like everyone says is their dead loved one visiting. My future dog? A cat would be cool, even though that's not my style. Not a snake, though; snakes are fucking creepy.

"My son? Yeah, like that's going to happen. Who knows, maybe someday I'll fucking grow up and be the man Lisa always wanted me to be.

"Lisa. Lisa and I will name our son for you. I promise. I love you, buddy."

God damn, man...

A TAP at the door and Jan's voice cause Mike to wipe his tears and blow his nose. "Yeah, Mom. It's open."

"Mike, you won't believe who is on the phone right now."

"The prison, again?" Squinted eyes proceed a shake of Mike's head.

"No. Sam. He's talking to Saul." Jan leans against the door for support as Mike races past her to the kitchen.

"Okay. Okay. Yes. Of course." Saul nods at Mike and smiles. "Wait, Sam. Hold on just a minute. Let me speak with Mike. Yes. Hold on."

"Mike. Sam thought he was dreaming last night when we spent time with him. He only realized it was real when he found my card with your name on it in his coat pocket. He wants our help. I will fill you in on the rest when I finish with Sam."

Words spin around Mike's head in the form of sentences and memories resembling Saul telling him that Sam wants help. Only then does he realize that his mom is leaning against him now for support. He wraps an arm around her shoulder and squeezes. Together, they absorb the one-sided conversation and attempt to remain calm as Saul continues talking to Sam.

Once he is finished, white teeth glimmer through a full smile on Saul's face. "This, my friends, is very good news. Sam woke up this morning with his face in the dirt and Joni propositioning him. She offered him a..." as he tries to form a decent explanation for the words he can't take back, he smiles at Jan. "A good time if Sam would just get her a hit of meth.

"Okay, that's not the good news." Saul shakes his head and clears his throat in response to the gaping faces in front of him. "The good news is that Sam said he vaguely remembers a promise he made to himself during one bad trip that if you came looking for him, he would do anything needed to get clean.

"He's asking for our help. I told him we would pick him up as soon as we could. I told him there were some things I needed to arrange first. We need to check with a local rehab to see if they have room and what their requirements are."

"Hope of East Tennessee," Jan removes a brochure from the top drawer near the phone and hands it to Saul. "I've already done all the research. I want Sam to be taken here. I kept their number for just this occasion.

"They're a twenty-eight-day program set in a residential neighborhood just three miles away from the Home Depot. The patients are not under lockdown but are carefully observed to ensure that rules are followed. Treatment mainly consists of lectures and twelve-step meetings, as well as individual and group therapy."

After reading the pamphlet, Saul agrees with the

choice. "In addition to having a roof over his head and three nutritious meals a day, I like the strict schedule and the fact that visitors are allowed as long as they don't interfere with meetings or progress.

"This is certainly a good place to start. I will find a local psychologist that has high recommendations for additional therapy. This could really work out well."

Saul dials the number and asks about admitting a new patient.

"THIS PLACE LOOKS TOTALLY different during the day," Mike admits as the BMW slows to a stop behind the Home Depot. "My God, I didn't see how much junk was piled here last night. Flames from the fire kept the reality literally in the dark." Mike spots Sam and nudges Saul, nodding in his direction.

Sam paces as if he is unsure where he belongs. With his hands tucked in his jeans, he stands still once he sees Mike and Saul get out of the car and start walking toward him.

"Sam. Hey, man. Are you ready to get out of here?" The question seems to confuse Sam. Glancing over his shoulder at the other men, he knits his eyebrows before lowering his head. Shoes that used to be white have turned brown with caked dirt.

Maybe he didn't realize what Saul said earlier. Maybe he thinks he will be able to get help but still live here.

"Uh, yeah, okay. Where are we going? I should let the guys know when I will be back, so they don't worry. We do that."

"Sam," Saul speaks in his tranquil psychologist voice. "You won't be coming back here. Isn't that what you want? You said you want help to get clean and be able to regain the respect of your family. That can't happen if you continue to live here."

"Fuck yeah, that's what I want. Of course, do you think I'm fucking stupid? Don't get in my shit, man. Don't fuck with me. We watch out for each other here. If you fuck with me, these guys will fucking kill you."

"Sam, are you high?" Aggression is one of the signs of being on methamphetamine and Saul is on high alert.

"You're fucking right I'm high. Joni fucked me right before you guys got here, too, because I scored for her. I couldn't let her use alone, that's disrespectful. At least someone is proud of me. At least someone thinks I can do something right in my life. At least I wanted to fuck her."

"Do you want us to come back, later, Sam or will you come with us now?" Saul asks with a calm voice. "The choice is yours. But before you answer, remember you promised yourself that if Mike came looking for you that you would do whatever it takes to get clean.

"At the place you're going, they will help you overcome the areas in your life, the things that happened to you, that drove you here. I understand why you turned to drinking and drugs to erase some bad memories in your childhood."

In awe of Saul's ability to remain cool and express the perfect amount of empathy, Mike admires his ability to push through Sam's tough exterior with sensible words. "You're not alone, my friend. So many people in your shoes have done the same thing."

"We have some news for you, Sam," Mike announces after a moment of silence. "Dominic is dead; he died last night. There is no reason to let him have a hold on you, anymore. Dominic is powerless in hell. It's time to put this life behind you."

Sam raises his eyes to Mike, then glances at Saul; tears clean a straight line down each side of his face.

Saul nods, "it is absolutely possible to heal and put horrible scenes of your youth to bed. There are so many people who love you and will support you while you're getting clean—Mike, your mom..."

Feeling the need to mention Steve, Mike continues. "Sam, don't you want to see your son? Steve needs you. He misses his dad and wants you to be around."

Dirt scatters from under Sam's shoes as he strides toward the road. He turns to stare at his brother. "Well, are you coming?" Sam asks.

Mike is ecstatic that his brother accepted his offer

to help, but that doesn't mean there won't be plenty of frustration and disappointments in the near future.

"THIS IS IT, Sam. I'm here with you. We can do this." Mike parks in the Hope of East Tennessee lot, opens the back door, and reaches for Sam. Love overpowers the stench as the brothers embrace.

As Jan enters the kitchen, Saul raises his head. "I am so honored to be a part of bringing this family back together. I have had many clients come to me for support with a homeless relative, but I rarely have a chance to help the person who is homeless. Situations like this rarely have a happy ending.

"Sam wants this; he honestly wants a better life and to earn the respect of his son and you. I truly believe that this will work out perfectly. I appreciate that you put your trust in me."

Distracted by her own thoughts, Jan flashes a quick grin before she responds. "Saul, I need to ask you something. Do we need to tell Steve about Dominic's death? He never knew him. He's only heard stories and knows he is in prison. He doesn't know he is the one that touched his dad; we only told him it was a very bad man. I'm concerned about how Steve will react to that bad man being my brother."

"If it comes up during discussions, you can decide how much you think is appropriate to explain. I don't think it's necessary to point out specifics. If nothing good can come from it, usually it's not worth bringing it up."

UNSURE why his heart races in anticipation, Mike leans against his vehicle in the school parking lot waiting for classes to end. As soon as Lisa steps into the sunlight, a golden halo shines behind her, cast by the sun slipping behind a cloud.

Oh, my God. Danny, how could I ever let this perfect woman escape? How could I ever make her cry? I swear I didn't mean to take her for granted. I swear I never will again. If she lets me, I will spend the rest of my life making it up to her.

Steve exits the door a minute later and lumbers down the steps, his face scrunched in a frown. Once he spots the BMW, a smile forms and his pace increases. Lisa follows him to Mike.

"Hey, Bud. Want a ride home?" Mike asks as he holds the passenger door open.

Steve emits a singsong, "Well, yeah," as he climbs into the front seat, closes the door, and begins playing with the radio controls.

"Come here, you." Mike reaches for Lisa and she snuggles into his hug. Rose scents bring Mike back to 2002. "God, you're gorgeous. I'm sorry, I hope you don't mind that I dropped by; I had to see you."

Lisa pulls back, stands on her tiptoes, and places a short but sweet kiss on Mike's lips. "Please don't ever apologize for wanting to see me." Her eyes search his picking up on the longing in his soul. Pleased with the result of her kiss, she smiles and backs away.

"How did you do last night? Did you find Sam?" Lisa peers around Mike to make sure Steve can't hear their conversation.

"We did." Mike keeps his voice low. "He is a mess, not at all the brother I had when we were young. I'm not sure if he will ever be the same. We took him to Hope of East Tennessee yesterday afternoon. He wants help and is determined to get clean. I can only pray that he doesn't escape back to the streets.

"My worst fear is that Sam will start to get help then fall off the wagon and break Steve's heart. And my mom's…again."

"If he wants this bad enough, Mike, he will make it happen. Sometimes all you need is a little nudge. Have faith."

"You're so smart." Mike places a light kiss on her nose and he senses Steve staring a hole in his back.

"Oh, and Uncle Dominic died early yesterday. We spent the day reflecting on Mom's family. I know Danny is at peace now, which is the most important thing in my eyes. We can talk about all that tomorrow. You were able to get a sub, yes? Steve is fine missing a day, yes? I have the best day planned for all of us."

"Yes and Yes. What are we doing? I'm so intrigued."

"Surprise." Mike winks and brushes his lips across hers. "We'll pick you up at 7:00 AM. Dress for warm weather."

Lisa watches the BMW drive away and wonders if she will be able to keep up with such a fast-paced life-style. With a sigh, she wraps her arms around herself and decides to enjoy the time she has with Mike. He is the only man that ever gave her butterflies. Still does.

JAN MOPS up the excess spaghetti sauce on her place with a piece of garlic bread and Steve grimaces; he doesn't like his food to touch. As Steve walks to the sink, Mike decides there is no time like the present to have a talk about Sam. He and Saul thought it would be best to discuss Steve's dad in a relaxed setting with everyone around, not corner him in his room.

"Steve, Saul and I have some good news for you. Come have a seat."

Easing himself down into his chair at the table, Steve tilts his head and asks, "What's up?"

"We found your dad. He decided to get help and is staying at Hope of East Tennessee for the next month or so. There is a lot going on that he needs to work through before he will be well enough to be back in your life, though.

"It will take some time, but I want to let you know that Saul and I are both here for you if you have any questions about what's happening. I will do anything I can to help you."

Silence.

"Steve?" Saul searches the face of the teenager in front of him. Senses pick up more than visual cues. Anger, sadness, curiosity all pass within seconds of each other.

"This isn't going to be easy on any of us, especially you," Mike continues. "Will you please say something? Tell me what's going through that mind of yours."

"Why did you do that? You're just going to leave in a few days, anyway. Why don't you just do your thing and let me do mine? I don't need your help. Leave me alone."

Screeches from the chair legs echo in the dining room as Steve pushes away. Heavy footsteps pound to the second level in the direction of the west bedroom.

"I thought he would be happy," Mike gapes at the chair where his nephew sat ten seconds earlier. "Saul, what can I do, what can I say to let him know this is a good thing? How can I get through to him?"

"Sometimes just listening and letting someone talk it out can help. Let him know you're open to discussing whatever is running through his mind. It doesn't have to be about his dad."

Saul's encouragement pushes Mike out of his seat. As he walks up the steps, Mike tries to convince himself that Steve will come around. After Mike taps on Steve's bedroom door, a small voice tells him to go away. The door is unlocked, so Mike enters anyway and sits in the desk chair.

"Steve, what can I do to help you? I'm a fantastic listener if you want to talk about it."

Staring at the ceiling from the bed, Steve tries to ignore Mike, but he doesn't ask him to leave.

"Look, I get it that your life is very different from your friends. Kids can be so cruel when a peer doesn't share the same lifestyle as them.

"Your dad made some terrible decisions early in his life and has paid dearly for them, as have you and the rest of this family. He is ready to make changes in his life and needs our help." Mike concentrates on keeping an even tone.

"It's not going to be easy, but your dad is committed to making things right. The one reason he agreed to be admitted to Hope is because he can't stand the thought of you hating him. He misses you more than anyone and wants to try to make it up to you."

Mike pauses before nudging, "Would you please tell me why you're so upset?"

A poster of Nino Schurter, Mountain Bike World

Champion, hangs on the wall behind Mike. Steve sits with his back against the headboard and focuses on the picture; his eyes glaze over in thought.

Because Steve has not responded, Mike decides it's time to leave and let the boy process his thoughts. As he reaches for the door, though, Steve starts to talk.

"Hearing about my dad and the way he lives just reminds me of what a loser I am. All the kids at school know where he lives and say he's a bum and that *those people* should just be executed. That's the real reason I kicked the shit out of Dave. It's embarrassing enough how it is, but..." A sigh mixed with a growl expresses Steve's frustration.

"Why did he leave me in the first place? How could someone choose drugs over their own kid? My mom couldn't stand me, so she left, first. Then my dad didn't want me, so he dumped me on Grandma. You're leaving after all this is over and it's just going to be me and Grandma again.

"What's the use? Why even bother? What if all this is for nothing and my dad decides that he likes his old life better than us and doesn't want to get better? Everything will just go back to the way it was, anyway. Then what?"

~

HEAT from the fireplace transforms the living room into a warm, cozy area to relax; it's been a rough couple of days and Mike thinks they all deserve a drink. Or two. Three glasses sit on the coffee table as Mike pours out of a bottle of wine from Paris.

"Saul, I want to thank you for all you have done for us in such a short period of time. You have gone above and beyond and I truly value your friendship. The way you are helping my mom, my brother, my nephew, and me is beyond what I could imagine.

"Thank you, from the bottom of my heart." Mike raises his glass and nods toward the man who has arranged much of Sam's recovery. Jan follows suit with watery eyes and a genuine smile.

"Ah, Mike. When friends need support, it's common for those closest to them to step up. You and I clicked from the first day we met. We understand each other. You are a kind person with a great heart and I am proud to call you my friend. Whatever I can do to help your wonderful family, I will." Saul nods and seals the sentiment with a clink of his glass.

Jan kicks off her slippers and tucks her feet under the blanket draped beside her on the couch. "Sam reminds me a little of your grandpa. He lost his family, too, but in a different way.

"No one knew what PTSD was back then. If they had a name for the reason so many veterans came back from Vietnam as completely different individuals, maybe some of our bravest Americans could have been saved.

"My mom divorced him not long after he got back. I was just six years old; Dominic was nine and gave Dad all kinds of hell. We could never understand why daddy wasn't coming home every night like in our friends' families. My mother didn't handle it well at all.

"Looking back, I can't say that I blame her. Dad was off drinking and spending time with other women. We didn't know what that meant, either, but we knew it wasn't something my mom liked. After she left him, she realized very quickly that she couldn't afford to raise us on her own. Six months later, we had another daddy."

"How did you adjust to a new family dynamic?" Saul wonders out loud.

"Well, let me just tell you that I am now convinced that my stepdad molested Dominic. He told me and my mom that he was being touched almost every night before bed, but we didn't believe him.

"He always had such a vivid imagination. My brother would tell incredibly detailed stories about the bears in the woods behind our house and how he crashed his bike riding down the road. There was never any evidence to collaborate his stories, never any proof, so we thought he was making it up.

"God, what I wouldn't do to go back to those days

and change things..." her voice trails off as Jan's eyes dance with the flames.

"How did Pops take it? Having a replacement?" Mike poured more wine in his mother's glass.

"Not good. But I honestly think he saw it coming and figured at least my mom was happier without him. He drank a lot. I mean a lot, as in I don't remember him being sober until I was married to your dad.

"One night when he had us for the weekend, he told some broken stories about what he did in 'Nam. I was completely disturbed, and still am. It changed our relationship forever...but for the better, somehow. After that, I could almost understand why he was so different and how things happened the way they did.

"I never had a chance to know my half-brother, Eugene."

"Wait. Mom. Did you say Eugene?" Mike perks up when his mother talks of a brother. "Pops mentioned him on Friday. I didn't think you knew about him. Did you ever meet him?"

"Unfortunately, we never had the chance to meet. It seems that I tried to find him too late. By the time I had the courage to look for him, he had already passed away. I discovered he was born to a woman who raised him in Virginia and he was a very talented kicker for the Detroit Lions. He never had a family of his own.

"At the time of his death, he lived in California, so I doubt we would have ever crossed paths." Wine swirls at the bottom of Jan's glass as she searches for answers to questions that are likely unanswerable.

Saul gazes at Mike with eyes wide open. He knows exactly what Mike is thinking.

"Mom. When did he pass away?" As he leans forward to hear her better, the wine glass almost slips out of Mike's hand.

"Gosh, Mike, it must be about five years ago, now. Why? What are you thinking?"

"Don't you see? Gene is the name of the man who I connected with at Red's. He was from Virginia and a kicker for the Detroit Lions. When he retired from football, he became a traveling salesman. The man who said that he felt we were soulmates; he thought I hung the moon.

"He is the man that left me his fortune when he died. Five years ago. Gene. Eugene?"

Jan gasps and raises her hand to her mouth. Tears form and begin to run down her cheeks.

"Gene was my uncle. God, that explains so much. He never told me."

Chapter 19
JANUARY 8, 2015

Security guards lead the group from Tennessee through the American Airlines Center in downtown Dallas. Fleece wraps around Lisa's shoulders along with Mike's arm as they follow Steve and Saul at a slight distance.

"I thought I was supposed to dress for warm weather. What the hell, Mike?" Her smirk eases his mind and he shakes his head.

"Hey, one would think that Texas in January might be warmer than thirty-eight degrees. You look fantastic in that dress, though. I love the free-flowing skirt."

A kiss in her hair relays his apology and he laces his fingers with hers as they walk.

French doors open into an oversized gathering area backstage. Steve's eyes dart around the room, taking in the sight. Two leather couches form an "L" in front of a glass coffee table in one corner, while six high-back chairs frame a rectangle oak dining table in another.

In the center of the room, two cowhide couches, end-tables at each side, sit on either edge of a cowhide rug. An eccentric coffee table is situated between the couches. Longhorns and barbed wire decorate the wall behind the bar and above a flat-screen at the far end of the room. Stools in the shape of saddles are positioned in front of the granite counter.

Smoky scents draw Mike's eye to one wall lined with a long table full of traditional barbecue and side dishes. Muffled country music plays as the crowd enters the stadium and finds their seats.

"Mike? Oh, my God! It's so great to see you." Alli closes the gap between herself and her mentor with an honest smile spread across her face. After a warm embrace and a kiss on her cheek, Mike releases his friend.

"What brings you to Dallas? We are in Dallas, right? I try to say the name of each city at least ten times before we go on stage. Dallas, Dallas, Dallas. You have no idea how embarrassing it is to say hello to Portland when you're in Orlando." Brunette curls bounce around Alli's face as she shakes her head and laughs at herself.

"Dallas, yes. Last I checked." Mike chuckles. "Hi, Alli. It's great to see you, too. We came here tonight just to see you and Charlie. My nephew, Steve, is a huge fan."

Unable to speak, starstruck, Steve nods as he tries not to drool.

Mike continues the introductions. "This is Lisa..."

"Lisa from Oakdale?" Alli doesn't wait for Mike to finish before she launches at her new best friend with open arms. A tight hug and a giggle complete the welcome.

"It's so nice to finally meet you. Mike has told so many stories about the concerts the two of you went to and how he came to love music so much. Britney and Justin were so hot back then. You're so lucky to have had Mike as your escort."

"It's great to meet you, too, Alli. You're right. I am lucky." Lisa leans into Mike without realizing she's doing it. The weight of his arm over her shoulder offers natural comfort.

"You remember Saul?" Mike nods toward his friend.

"How could I forget? Best shrink in L.A. This guy is one of the reasons Charlie and I can write songs with a positive message. Nice to see you, Saul. Come, sit. We still have an hour before we have to prep. Charlie will be here in a few minutes, she is making the nightly call to her man. Can I get you a drink?"

"You still don't have people to do that for you?" Mike helps Alli gather beers, wine, and a Pepsi.

"Come on, Mike. You know me better than that." Alli smiles as Charlie makes her entrance.

"I thought I heard a familiar voice. Mike, my friend, how the hell are ya?" Lipstick stains Mike's cheek after Charlie plants her customary greeting. "Oops, sorry."

"Charlie, you'll never guess who this is?" Hand in hand, the girls lead the way to Lisa, Steve, and Saul, leaving Mike to carry the drinks.

"No freaking way! Lisa?"

"How did you..."

"I overheard." Charlie winks and leans in for an embrace. "So nice to meet you."

Long blonde locks fall to one side as Charlie tilts her head and puts on her best sparkling smile. "Steve, right? What's up?" The simple greeting and chin lift leave the teen speechless.

After settling on the couches in the center of the room, Lisa asks the girls how they got their start. "I've heard so much about your lives, but I'm curious where you started. How did you get the bug for playing for crowds? Wasn't that intimidating?" Elbows on her knees, Lisa leans forward, anticipating Charlie's response.

"My mom bought me a guitar for Christmas the same year Alli and I started hanging out. I was infatuated with George Lynch and wanted to play just like him. Perfecting "Mr. Scary" was my ultimate goal. I introduced Alli to the guitar and after about four minutes, she decided that singing was more in her nature."

"Yeah, I sucked." Alli laughs, good-naturedly, and continues their practiced story. "After talking two of our friends into joining our band and practicing covers for a year, we landed our first gig at this hole-in-the-wall in our hometown, Brooklyn, Michigan.

"Place was called Callahan's and it smelled like ass. Big dance floor, sketchy crowd. A friend's mom helped us reach out to bigger bars and we landed gigs in larger, more upscale towns like Dexter, Novi, Royal Oak, and Birmingham.

"After another year or so, we finally got enough of a following to land small bars in Detroit, which scared the shit out of my mom. She felt better when we played in Ann Arbor. Even came to see us a few times. Honestly, as the crowds gradually grew, it got easier to be in front of more people the more we played."

"From there, we went on the road for a while, trying to stay in warm states during the winter, and eventually landed in L.A." Charlie resumes. "We heard about this guy who opened a couple bars and helped aspiring bands make it to the big time. We thought 'what the hell?' and looked for the infamous Mr. Allen." Leaning back with crossed legs and a glass of wine in hand, Charlie toasts in Mike's direction. "The rest is history."

"You walked into Lisa's with such confidence and

poise, Danny elbowed me in the ribs and said 'Dude, these girls got something special.' He was so right." The memory of Danny's declaration brings a smile to Mike's lips, thankful to appreciate the fond memories.

"You found them at Lisa's? With Danny?" Lisa was not able to stop her tears. Her index finger swipes away one that falls. "I'm sorry to get emotional, but I had no idea. The fact that you named a bar after me, for one, is incredibly touching, but that Danny was with you when these girls reached out to you for help..." her voice trails off.

"Steve, we wouldn't be here if it weren't for your uncle and Danny, God rest his soul," Charlie says.

Alli joins in Charlie's toast with a Coors Light in her hand. "Thanks to them, we made it. We had no idea what we were doing until this guy took us under his wing. He gave us the best opportunity, introduced us to the honest people in the industry, and held our hands every step of the way.

"The best part is, he's so selfless that he didn't even take a cut. You really have to be careful in this industry; it seems like everyone is out for your money. Except Mike." Turning her focus from Steve to Mike, Alli's offers a genuine smile.

"All of this is because of you. If we spent the rest of our lives trying, we could never thank you enough. If we can ever do you a favor, anything, you better call."

"HELLO, DALLAAAAS!"

Charlie follows Alli onstage with fingers strumming her guitar to their most recent number one hit, "Lemonade." Both girls are dressed in leather pants: Alli in her signature tank-top and Charlie with a bright yellow, oversized, see-through shirt over a black sports bra. Fireworks explode before multi-colored lights flash in sync with the beat of the drums.

"Are you ready for a party?" Alli asks the crowd of 20,000 plus. The roar is so loud Mike has a hard time hearing the lead singer speak into the microphone.

These days it's rare to find a musical group with such a positive message. Heaven Scent became so popular so fast that every concert sells out in minutes.

Alli begins to sing in her signature steely tone, unique and always on key. A slight twang sneaks through, even though the girls are from the Midwest. Mike remembers why he pushed for this group to be signed and is elated to be the person who introduced them to this world.

A grin stretches across his face and Lisa can't resist planting a kiss on his cheek.

> All my teachers said I would fail that I
>   had no future
> They thought they knew me, but they
>   were so wrong

Just because I came from nowhere
    didn't mean I wasn't strong
I was a little shit with a bad attitude,
    but those days are all a blur

Life game me lemons, lemons, lemons
And I made lemonade

Sun shining on my face, sunglasses give
    me shade
My girls swimming in the pool getting
    a chlorine marinade
We'll all be smokin' hot ready to set this
    town ablaze
While I make my lemon, lemon,
    lemonade

ONLY A FEW FEET from the stage, Mike's group is immersed in the full Heaven Scent experience. Heat from the lights brings beads of sweat to Saul's forehead and the beat of the drums reverberates in Mike's chest. Steve hasn't blinked since Charlie strutted in front of him, he can't take his eyes off the rocker. He nods his head to the beat and begins to sing along.

Speakers positioned at the corners of the stage blare a guitar solo that no band can match, men or women. Music reaches their ears at a volume so loud the friends don't attempt to talk.

Honest lyrics, written by young girls breaking through into a man's world, touch the crowd. Each song is uplifting and positive, a promise Charlie and Alli made on day one. If they were going to do this, it would be to help people through hard times. Hard work and persistence paid off with fame and success.

Danny, you would be so proud of these girls. Remember when they first played at Lisa's? They were so young and so green. You were right. They do have something special. I know you're watching them. I know you're here.

I miss the old days of going anywhere and everywhere to watch a great concert. Or a horrible one. Mike laughs to himself. *Yeah, there were some bad bands, weren't there?*

"This next song is special to us in so many ways. It was our first single and the song we played the night we were discovered by Mike Allen. After years of denials, Mike saw something in us and believed we had what it takes to make it.

"For those of you who know our story, you know about Mike. Super cool thing is, he flew out here tonight to enjoy the show. Thanks, Mike. We love ya, man. This one's for you."

While Mike's friends belt out the beloved words of their first hit, his nephew sings along with the chorus.

Now it's time, time to believe
Believe, believe, believe Marie

She won't settle, won't give up
She's finally, finally, finally free

Persistence will pave the road
Lead to joy, love, and success
She has to do this on her own
Push away feelings of distress

Hold your head up, don't back down
She repeats the mantra every day
Determined to follow all her dreams
One day she'll live in Monterrey

Charlie rips the guitar riff as she struts across the stage, stopping in front of Steve. She points at him and mouths 'for you.' Her eyes close as she leans her head back, long hair moves to the beat of the background drums. Steve stares without blinking the entire length of the solo.

Lisa nudges Mike and smiles before she catches his lips on hers.

Through closed eyes, the music washes over Mike like a wave on a moonlit beach. Lisa stands in front of him and leans her weight against his chest; his arms wrap around her waist. His love for music and his love for this woman is all he needs for the rest of his life.

Warmth fills Mike's heart and he thinks to himself, *this is what it's all about.*

HEADPHONES COVER STEVE'S ears as he expresses, for the hundredth time, how much he loves Charlie. "I can't believe you know them! How fricking cool!!! Charlie is so hot! The way she rocks that guitar, mmm-mmm. She's a goddess, I swear." Tired eyes drift closed as his head bops to Heaven Scent's new album.

"That kid is so darn sweet, I swear." Lisa whispers and smiles at Mike. "You think he would enjoy concerts like we did when we were just a few years older than him?"

"Without a doubt." Mike's fingertips caress Lisa's cheek and she leans into his touch. "Thank you, Mike, for today. This was the best trip. Charlie and Alli are wonderful—such great influences."

Mike's fingers lace under her hair and encourage Lisa's face to move toward his. Passion shows in his eyes as he whispers on her lips. "I've been waiting all night to do this." Soft kisses quickly grow deeper and Lisa pulls back before the desire increases.

Foreheads touching, they slow their breathing as smiles spread across their faces. One word is spoken at the same time.

"Steve."

After the couple repositions themselves on the couch under a blanket, Lisa leans her head on Mike's shoulder, entwined fingers connect them.

"I can't believe that Gene was your uncle. How, just...odd. Do you think he would have told you eventually?" Lisa turns to search Mike's eyes for understanding.

"Honestly? I don't know. I would like to think that he would have told me, but once we discovered we had such a connection, would it have been awkward? I wonder if we were so comfortable together because he looked for our family and knew who I was or because we were so much alike.

"There are so many unanswered questions; it's so weird to think that he had this secret. Maybe he just wanted to be close to his family. I wonder if he would have asked about his dad at some point or if he was satisfied knowing that everyone was happy. Maybe he thought he would disrupt our life if he told us the truth."

Silence fills the space long enough for Lisa to close her eyes and drift into a dream about being on a private jet with her boyfriend after a concert in Dallas.

"I have to go back to California tomorrow but will be back on Saturday. Will you join me for dinner when I return?"

"Mmm-hmm."

S unsets in Tennessee range from red and orange to pink and purple; the mountains are always a deep blue to black. Sometimes the fog settles between the ridges as if the hills are smoldering. At least that's what Allen McKay remembers. Each time he witnessed a beautiful sky as the sun sank behind the Smokies, Allen chalked it up to God's paintbrush.

"Pops, wow. That sunset is absolutely beautiful." Mike's head tilts to get a better look at his grandfather's latest painting. "Is that from the overlook in Oakdale?"

"I used to take your grandmother there to get away from the kids for an hour or two. She would pack a picnic and set our place at the table—well, it's more of a rock bench, but we made it work. Before we married, it was our place to meet in secret. Her German parents were not keen on their daughter

253

dating an Irish man. We even carved our initials in a tree. AM + AS.

"After we split, I continued to go to our spot at least once a week. I never forgave myself for the way I treated her after the war. Don't blame her a bit for getting as far away from me as she could. Wonder if that old rock is still there?" Allen's gaze leads out the window, but Mike has a feeling he is deep in memories.

"You'll be happy to hear that it's still there, Pops. I just sat on it with my love last week, such a magical place. Lisa has this exact view that she captured in a photograph last year hanging over her fireplace. After we split up, she kept returning to our spot, too."

Allen squints and tilts his head to ask Mike a silent question.

"Lisa and I used to go there during high school when we wanted to be alone. We even carved our initials in a tree under AM + AS. She will be thrilled that the mystery of the 'other' initials has been solved."

With a nod and a small smile, Allen turns back to the painting and raises his brush.

"Hey, Pops. What happens to all the rest of your paintings? Do you sell them or give them away?"

"Your mom said she has a special room where her favorites are displayed."

"Well, I need to ask her about that. Listen, we came here to tell you some news. The last time we visited, you mentioned a girl that said she had a son, your son. Eugene."

"What about Eugene?" Allen snaps then softens. "I don't know any more than I told you, already."

"Well, somehow Mom knew about Eugene and started looking for him only to find out that he passed away. I'm sorry.

"She told me everything she found out about him: where he grew up, his profession, where he lived. I didn't put two and two together until a couple days ago. Remember the man that used to visit me at the bar? The one who left me his fortune? Gene LaPort.

"Mom and I think that Gene was my uncle. The man that was so generous to me was your son. Eugene."

Without taking his eyes off the painting, Allen sinks onto the stool behind him. After the words sink in, he blinks and turns to Mike. "Eugene? He found you."

"Yes, Pops. He was a fun, kind, wonderful man. We used to have great conversations and adventures each time he was in town. We clicked right away and I always thought we had a unique connection. Now I understand the reason."

"Well. I don't know what to say. It makes me happy that you were able to know him and that he was a good man. I'm sorry to hear that he passed away; thank you for telling me. Mike? Do you think that is who covered the bill for me to live here until my last day? Your mom swears it wasn't her."

"Wow, I didn't know that had been arranged. I bet you're right. If I find out, I will certainly let you know."

"THANKS FOR THE RIDE, man. I always thought about buying a plane; this is hands-down the best way to travel. Call me when you get back to Tennessee and keep me updated on everything, okay?"

A smirk hides Mike's pride. "Hey, before you go, can you do me a favor?" Sun shines in Mike's eyes causing him to squint and reach for his sunglasses.

"Anything, friend."

"Could you ask one of your lawyer friends to investigate Gene's will? I would really like to tell Pops if Gene covered his living expenses."

"You got it." Saul reaches for Mike's hand and is pulled into an embrace.

A BLACK MERCEDES, identical to Mike's, sits outside the garage, off to one side, in the driveway. The three garage doors are closed, so Mike wonders who is visiting. After taking in the plates, he realizes it's not a visitor.

Why the hell is my Mercedes parked outside? Fucking Rebecca must not have moved out. Today has already started to suck.

The driver opens the car door, places Mike's bag next to the garage near the keypad entry, and leaves without speaking, as predicted.

Once the garage door is open and Mike walks to the space where his Mercedes is usually parked, he understands why his car has been moved.

A Bentley occupies the space; Mike does not own a Bentley. Plates that read "Joe Ben" tell more than Mike cares to know.

Seriously, Bec?

Amused and annoyed, Mike allows a grin and shakes his head as he walks through the kitchen. He stops as Senator Joe Benjamin comes into view. With the newspaper in front of his face, he is not aware that Mike enters the house.

"Hey, Joe."

"Mike." The newspaper falls to the table as the Senator, wrapped in only a robe, begins to stand. "Well, this is awkward."

"Where's your girlfriend?"

"I suspect she's still in the shower."

Stairs pass under Mike's feet as if he's in a dream. He's not upset that his wife is cheating; that's not the point. Rebecca didn't hide her affairs very well and Mike had a feeling that she spent time with other men. What bothers him most is that he asked her to leave, on more than one occasion, and she made a conscious decision to be a squatter.

"Did you come back for thirds, lover?" Rebecca giggles before she realizes it's Mike that enters the room. As she turns to him, she wipes the white powder from under her nose.

"What part of 'get the fuck out of my house' wasn't clear?"

"Michael. I've been so worried about you." Three large steps close the space between them as Rebecca, wearing only a thin silk robe, reaches for her husband.

"You're making yourself look like an idiot. Do you think I didn't see your booty call by my breakfast nook? Just get the fuck out. Now." Two steps back put enough space between them that she can't touch him. "Don't make me get the police involved. It won't look good for your image."

Plump lips part as if to speak, but before she is able to coo another excuse, Mike cuts her off. "Look, Bec, you signed for the divorce papers last week. I know you received them. I really don't care if you read through it or not, but if you didn't, that's your own fault.

"Clearly stated in the paperwork is that if you sign for the registered mail and didn't respond or refute within three business days, you agree with everything that is written. I gave you five business days. The divorce is final. It's over. Get the fuck out."

"Divorce? Michael, what are you talking about?"

The silk belt releases and the robe separates, showing the space between her breasts. Painted fingertips, on one hand, trace a line down to her navel; the other hand moves the robe off one shoulder revealing one perfect C cup.

"Your lover is downstairs and you're trying to seduce me. You are certifiable."

"I can call him up and you can both have me. I've always wanted to have a threesome." The robe pools at Rebecca's feet and smooth, creamy skin covers a thin but muscular body. She steps closer to Mike and licks her lips. Orange blossom and vanilla assault Mike's nose.

"You're sick." Mike snaps as he leaves the room.

Joe and his Bentley squeal out of the driveway as Mike pulls his cell phone from his pocket.

Five minutes later, LAPD arrives and two officers meet Mike in the driveway. He shows them the divorce paperwork and advises that there is an intruder. Yes, she happens to be his ex-wife, but she refuses to leave.

"Not to worry, Mr. Allen. My partner and I will handle this for you."

Rebecca appears in the doorway with her purse and overnight bag. Sunglasses cover her eyes. One of the officers carries an oversized suitcase to her car and puts it in the trunk. She refuses to meet Mike's gaze as she drives out of his life, forever.

Patterned cement meets Mike's comfortable

sneakers as he makes his way across the back patio. His favorite view from this house is from the bar next to the hot tub attached to the pool.

On a good day, he enjoys a cold Coors Light as the sun warms his face and arms. This day turned into just the opposite. The beer has not been restocked in the mini-fridge; all there is to drink is wine and water.

Ahh, Danny. Brother, I miss you. I'd give anything to dial your number right now, so I could rant and rave about this day. I guess I don't really need a phone anymore, do I? Well, you witnessed it all, but can you also read my mind?

Yeah. I'm out. There isn't anything keeping me in L.A. Everyone I love is in Oakdale. I have some work to do, don't I? Sometimes I wish to God I didn't know now the things I didn't know then.

"Mr. Allen, how are you? I'm so pleased that you have returned." Anita, Mike's housekeeper, appears beside him with a cold Coors Light.

"Hello, Anita." The icy bottle is refreshing in his hand. Mike takes a long pull before continuing. "You always could read my mind. I'm afraid that things are going to change around here."

Although she is sad to lose Mike as a customer, she gladly accepts a sizable severance.

"It's okay, Mr. Allen. Rebecca was a witch. I need to see my son and his family in New Jersey before I start something new, so the compensation will help me immensely."

PHOTOGRAPHERS BUZZ AROUND THE HOUSE, garage, and property capturing every angle of every space in every room. An overly excited realtor gathers details from Mike to include in the listing for the sale of his home. After negotiating on what should stay with the house and how the listing should read, they decide on a price and sign the contract.

Phone calls to alert Mike's staff of the changes prove to be a difficult task. He cares for each of these people, deeply. They have taken care of him in their own way and are considered friends. His chef, Andre, declines the invitation to move to Tennessee but accepts a reference to a friend Malibu.

Mike contacts a moving company and arranges to have the contents of his home packed and shipped to a storage facility in Knoxville. Anita offers to ensure the safety of all items within the home until it sells.

The same moving company ships vehicles in enclosed trailers, so Mike arranges for three of his vehicles to be delivered to his mother's home. The others will be sold by his chauffeur and the money direct deposited into Mike's account.

Mike invites his pilot for one last dinner and informs him of the situation. "Jason, if you want to move to Tennessee, I would love to keep you on my payroll."

"Boss, I don't have anything keeping me in California. You know me, I'm always up for an adventure. I have really enjoyed the last two weeks in Tennessee and would love to give it a go. Just need to make some phone calls."

"Whatever you need. I will continue to keep up my end of our current agreement and cover any moving expenses. Just let me know who to make the check out to. Tomorrow, let's land in Knoxville, so we can set up a hanger for the big girl."

"You got it."

Chapter 21
JANUARY 10, 2015

Blue lights from the guest room alarm clock reflect on the ceiling. Three thirteen AM. For a moment, Mike forgets that he is not in Tennessee. The phone sitting on the end table buzzes for the third time.

Who the hell is calling at this hour?

Chills run through his body when 'Mom' appears on his cell phone screen. "Mom? What's wrong? Are you okay?"

"Mike. I'm so worried. Stevie is gone." Sobs echo like howling on the other end of the phone.

Careful to not add to his mother's stress, Mike inhales and focuses on keeping his tone smooth and steady. "Mom, I need you to breathe. I need you to talk to me."

"But Stevie..."

"It's okay to take a few minutes to figure out what

to do. We must remain calm. Tell me exactly what happened." Covers fall off the bed as Mike stands to pull on sweats and a t-shirt.

A slow exhale proceeds Jan's shaky words. "He went over to Chase's house last night and hasn't come home. His bed is still made and he's not answering his cell phone.

I called Chase and his mom said the boys were together most of the day, but Steve didn't stay the night. His other friends haven't seen him, either; I have called everyone I can think of. Where else he could be?" A gasp takes the place of a breath. "Mike, please tell me he's okay."

"Yeah, he's okay. We'll find him. Let's think this through. Obviously, I can't do much from California." Whimpers come through the phone. "Listen, mom, you need to push away the fear for a few minutes. You need to think. You need to act. Keep it together until I can get there, okay?"

Another deep breath and Jan's words are calm. "Okay. Okay, Mike. I can do this. For Stevie."

"I need you to call the police, then call Daniel Jones. I will text you his number. Call them right now, then call me back right away. It will be fine, Mom. We'll find him."

His phone disconnects and Mike gazes out the window, taking in the view of the Pacific. This is probably the only thing he will miss from California.

God help me. Help my mom. Help Stevie. Danny, if you can lend a hand, I could really use your support.

"Lisa, hi. I'm sorry it's so early. I need your help."

AT THE AIRPORT IN MALIBU, Mike's driver parks next to the Jet, as he has done hundreds of times in the past. During the ten-minute drive, Mike explained that he is moving to Tennessee and has referred him to of a couple friends that could use a dedicated driver.

Powerful arms wrap around Mike and pull him into a short hug as the driver embraces him one last time. "It's been a pleasure knowing you, my friend. Keep the Lincoln." He pushes the title to the car and ten one-hundred-dollar bills in the driver's hand, smiles, and nods his goodbye.

Steps covered with non-slip strips lead the way to the threshold of Mike's Gulfstream. Jason greets him inside and senses tension. "Mike, good morning. Is everything okay? You seem a little stressed." A nod dismisses any conversation and Jason understands that his mission is to fly Mike home. Again.

Negative scenarios dance through Mike's head and he pushes them away with Danny's help.

It's ridiculous to think about my nephew lying dead in a ditch along the side of the road, right? He wasn't walking along the side of a dark dirt road where some drunk guy hit him and ran off? I'm sure he hasn't overdosed or been kidnapped. Right? He hasn't been shot in a drive-by, and he certainly didn't get in a bar fight and end up stabbed to death.

What the hell, Danny. Where could he possibly be? Please tell me he didn't run away because of me.

The four-hour flight feels like sixteen.

BACK IN TENNESSEE, Coach Smalls opens the door to the Lincoln, not wasting any time as he takes Mike to Oak Ridge. "Your mom and Lisa are waiting at the house in case Steve shows up. Daniel called in a favor and has the entire Oak Ridge police department searching for him."

"Thank you for being here, Coach. I really appreciate your time. What can we do that the police aren't? Do you have any weird-ass ideas on where a thirteen-year-old boy would go?" A leather headrest supports Mike as he closes his eyes.

"I've been thinking about that, Mike. What happened in his life in the past week that would either drive him away or make him look for somewhere to be safe?"

Eyes pop open as the thought travels from Mike's brain to his mouth. "Sam. We found Sam and he agreed to go to rehab. I told Steve where he is staying, so if he went there looking for his dad, they would have called." Thinking it through doesn't help Mike solve the riddle. "It has to have something to do with Sam. But what?"

Mike's cell phone buzzes in his hand. He answers without looking at the screen. "Mike. Steve is home. He's okay. He's home." Jan whispers the last words.

"Oh, thank God. Thank you, God. Mom. I'll be there in five minutes. We'll talk then." The sigh from Mike triggers Coach to fill the space with comforting conversation.

"Steve's home?"

A nod from the back seat confirms Coach's suspicion.

"Mike, that's so great. I'm thrilled. I'm sure he was just out having some fun like you and Danny used to do when you were his age. Remember when the two of you stayed out all night fishing? Your mom about had a conniption fit when she found out that you didn't actually drown."

A deep laugh escapes as Mike's shoulders relax. "How do you remember all this stuff? God, it's been a hundred years. She was a wreck back then; I can't imagine what she went through last night.

"So much has changed in the past twenty years. I tried so hard to fight off all the negative possibilities. I can't imagine what was going through my mom's head."

GARLIC AND OREGANO reach Mike's nose and laughter reaches his ears as he enters his mother's house. Lasagna ingredients cover the granite countertop, pots and pans covered with soap suds fill the sink, and Jan and Steve sit at the bar like nothing happened. Cards are stacked between them and spread in their hands like a paper folding fan.

"Hey, Mom. Steve." Each of them glances at Mike between giggles. "What's so funny?"

"Did you know that your foot is as long as the space between your wrist and elbow?" Steve quizzes his uncle. "Seriously. It is. Grandma just tested the theory and it's true."

"You okay, Steve?"

"Yeah. Wanna hear a funny story?" Eyebrows raise above Mike's eyes at the same time as Steve's chin lifts. Cards fold in his hand and he turns to face his uncle.

Mike answers with a nod.

"So, I was at the library last night and..."

"Wait," Mike interrupts. "You were at the library. You seriously want me to believe that?"

"Mike, it's true," Jan confirms the alibi. "The library is closed on Saturday, but the librarian had some organizing to do and stumbled upon Steve. Literally."

"I fell asleep researching drug addiction and homelessness. I wanted to learn about why my dad is the way he is—what he went through and how it changed him. Anyway, the librarian tripped over me on her way to turn on the lights. Scared the shit out of both of us."

"Speaking of scaring the shit out of someone, your grandma and I..." Jan cuts off Mike with her best 'mom' look, so Mike changes course, "...were totally freaked out by all the birds that have decided to make the backyard their home this winter."

DOSBRO'S Mexican restaurant is one of the more popular in Oak Ridge. It's not expensive, but the food is known as the best. Before Mike had money, he only dreamed of dining anywhere he desired. He and Lisa would search for the most economical places to eat, usually finding a decent hole in the wall.

After learning that hiring personal chefs is expected of rich folk, dining out lost all its allure. Andre creates the most flavorful and nutritious meals Mike has ever experienced. That is until he tasted what Lisa and Jacques created.

"What's good here?" Mike wonders out loud.

"I'm not sure, I've never been. Mexican food is all the same, though, isn't it? Meat, onions, spices, rice, beans all wrapped in a tortilla. Just served in a different position on the plate." Lisa tilts her head.

Menus sit between them and Lisa reaches for

one. "See, a burrito, taco, chimi, and quesadilla all made of the same ingredients, different delivery."

"You're right. How did you get so smart, Miss Johnson? So observant?"

Rolling her eyes, Lisa changes the subject. "You know, it would be easier for you to watch over Steve if you were here. Your mom was scared today; I'm glad you asked me to go be with her. I think keeping her busy helped. We did some fantastic baking and had a really great conversation.

"Everything that has happened since you've been home has been a step in the right direction for your entire family. Sam is in rehab and excited about reconnecting with his son, Steve is curious and educating himself on the effects of drug addiction. He understands how his dad went off the deep end and can work towards forgiving him.

"I'm sure your mother would love to have you home, nearby. She loves you so much and misses you terribly. And Grandpa Allen, he misses you but would never think to admit it." Lisa glances at Mike and offers a shy smile. "I've missed you, too."

"Hmm." With a smirk, Mike tilts his head. Flickers of light reflect in his eyes as Mike stares at the love of his life. "You've missed me?"

Heat rises to Lisa's cheeks as she senses his desire. Feeling the need to slow his passion, she asks a question that she understands will be difficult but has been on her mind. "You're so patient with Steve. Why didn't you have kids?"

Caught off guard, Mike leans back in his chair. "Well. For starters, Rebecca is too vain. She said it would ruin her body to have an alien growing to the size of a watermelon inside her. She only cares about herself anyway. I knew our relationship wouldn't last and it's not fair to put a child through a nasty divorce.

"Not only did I have to experience parent's going through a divorce but so many people in L.A. use their kids as pawns. Look at Tiger and Elin, Charlie and Denise, Tom and Katie, not to mention Alec and Kim. That situation is a train wreck."

"Makes total sense," Lisa nods.

Silence grows close to uncomfortable before Lisa pushes the subject again. "So, are you going to stay?"

A hearty chuckle accompanies a genuine smile. "You want me to stay, don't you?"

"I do, Mike."

I like how that sounds. I've waited so long to hear those words come from that beautiful woman.

"I have something to tell you." Red wine swirls in his glass and Mike watches the legs drift down the side and gather into itself.

Lisa raises her eyebrows in anticipation.

"I filed divorce papers the Monday after Christmas." Unsure if Lisa's response will be shock, pleasure, or anger, Mike hesitates to meet her eyes.

"That's the day after we saw each other again." A glimmer of hope reflecting from Lisa reassures Mike.

"Yes." He smiles and adds, "It's final. I went back to L.A. to tie up some loose ends. I knew it was going to happen but wasn't in any rush until I saw you. I knew that I didn't want anything giving me a reason to not be with you."

"Mike, I don't know what to say."

"No need to say anything. Look," Mike moves closer to the table and reaches for Lisa's hand. "I never let myself get close to anyone after we broke up. You are the only one that I have ever thought truly deserved my entire heart. I knew it then and I know it now.

"I blew it back then, but I would give anything to make up for lost time." Not taking his eyes off her, Mike raises her hand to his lips and places a delicate kiss on soft skin. "So, tell me. How is it that you never married?"

"Well," she takes a moment to think about how to phrase her response. "I've had a couple opportunities but never quite met anyone that was as good to me as you were. Are. I guess I ruined everyone else for me." Lisa sticks out her tongue and Mike knows she is only half-joking.

Chapter 22

JANUARY 11, 2015

Ninety-eight canvases covered with the same image in a variety of colors hang on the walls of, what Jan calls, "the Art Room." More paintings are held up with props on tables, a group of over-flow prints without frames sit on the floor and lean against the walls. Anna McKay's likeness is captured from every view one would imagine possible.

Other paintings lie in the closet, visions from her father's torrid past. The war continues to haunt Allen and the way he expels the demons is through his paintbrush. Those images are not what Jan chooses to view but she respects the need for her father to create and save them.

In the far corner sits an oversized, stuffed chair, turned at such an angle that each painting is visible. Steam rises off the coffee in Jan's mug as she lifts it to her lips and blows. Each time Jan relaxes in this chair, she senses love from her mother as if the paint emits emotion.

Sunday is her usual day to spend time with her mom and reflect on the events in her life for which she is thankful. Apple cinnamon scent from a wax burner reminds Jan of days spent baking pies with her mom.

Walls a shade called Cinder Rose bring back memories of picnics at sunset. Her mom would take Jan and Dominic to the overlook when her dad was "away" to witness God painting the sky with a beautiful sunset.

A painting of the view from the overlook lives in the center of the west wall. Allen painted the exact sunset scene that her mother loved so much. Jan's thoughts wander to a time when her mother repeated the story of how Allen proposed to Anna at their rock bench.

"Mom, are you in here?"

Mike hasn't been inside this room yet and pushes the door open, pausing before crossing the threshold. His late grandmother's likeness surrounds him and watches from multiple areas within the room.

"So, this is the room Pops was talking about." Slow steps in a circle allow Mike to take in the entire ambiance. "Phenomenal. Are there more?"

Without speaking, Jan uncurls her feet from under her and takes three steps to the closet. With pursed lips, she nods to her son and lowers her head before opening the door.

Mike understands the somber mood as the 'Nam scene from last week catches his eye at the front of a stack. His mother organized, labeled, and stored each canvas thoughtfully. "Do you keep them all?"

"I do. Daddy asked me to, so I honor his request. Obviously, I hang the paintings of Momma, but the others I date and keep orderly in the closet. I haven't looked at them since."

Mike puts his arm around her shoulders; Jan welcomes the support and leans into her son. "Maybe one day I will donate or sell them, but I can't image who would want such gruesome images."

ALUMINUM FOIL COVERS the leftover fried chicken on the plate Mike sets in the refrigerator. Full from another incredible meal inspired by Paula Dean, Jan and Steve remain at the table, sipping the last of their milk. Muted words and laughter fill the air, the activities of the past couple of days are behind them.

Mike's cell buzzes on the counter. "Are Jan and Steve with you?" Saul blurts out at the same time Mike says, "Hello."

"Yes," Mike chuckles. "We've just finished an early dinner. Everyone is still at the table. What's up?"

"Mike, put me on speakerphone, please. I think everyone will want to hear what I discovered."

After he sits at the table and signals to his family

that they need to hear this, Mike taps the speaker button and announces to Saul that they are listening.

"Jan, Steve, hello. Listen, I have some very interesting news. Good news." Saul lets out an unexpected laugh. "Great news. You won't believe it."

"Saul, buddy, get on with it. The suspense is killing us. What's going on?"

"You asked if I would look into Gene's will. It's public record at this point, so it wasn't difficult to get my hands on it. Mike, you wondered if he was the one who arranged for your grandfather to live out the remainder of his days in Canterfield; you were correct. Gene left more than enough money in an account that automatically pays the rent every month."

"That's fantastic news, Saul, but I would hardly consider it something I wouldn't believe." Shaking his head, he glances at his mother who wears a smile with watery eyes.

"You haven't let me finish. There's more. Gene also left a large sum of money in a trust that has yet to be claimed. The name of the beneficiary is Samuel Higgenbottom. Sam inherited two million dollars."

Jan's gasp proceeds Steve's cheer and Mike's laughter. "What," "You're kidding," and "Oh, my God," fill the receiver of the phone and reach Saul simultaneously. The three stand and hug, Steve jumps and punches the air, Jan's hands cover her mouth, and Mike raises his eyes to the heavens.

Thank you, Uncle Gene.

SUNDAY'S VISITING hours at Hope end at six-o-clock, so Mike makes a phone call to ensure he has permission to meet with his brother this soon after being admitted. Keys jingle in his hand as he reaches for his leather jacket. Light from the kitchen illuminates Steve's back as he stands in front of the sliding glass doors, watching the bird feeder.

"Hey, Steve. Do you want to go with me to tell your dad the good news? I know he will be thrilled to see your face. Although, it might be a bit uncomfortable at first, for both of you. But, hey, you gotta start somewhere, right?"

At first, Mike thinks maybe he didn't speak loud enough to break through his nephew's thoughts. When he clears his throat to try again, Steve turns to face him.

Tear-streaked cheeks are highlighted by a toothy smile. "Yeah, you gotta start somewhere. I'm nervous, but I wanna see my dad." Cotton soaks up the tears as Steve wipes his face with the arm of his sweatshirt and a sigh signal that this moment has been a long time coming.

"When Grandma and I talked last night, I told her I was embarrassed by my dad and the way he chooses to live. I am, but that doesn't mean I don't still want to be his son. I don't know how many times I've prayed to God asking for him to figure shit out and get clean. For him to think of how his life affects me and Grandma instead of just thinking about himself."

"You're pretty darn smart, Steve. I'm afraid I haven't given you enough credit. I hope you know I am extremely proud of you and the way you handle yourself. Your grandmother loves you so much and wants nothing more than for your dad to figure shit out, too."

WITH ONLY FORTY-FIVE minutes until visiting hours end, Mike and Steve climb the steps to the house where Sam lives. The intake coordinator greets them at the door, settles them in a meeting room, and excuses herself to find Sam.

A pleasant scent proceeds a tall, clean-shaven, thin man with short dirty blond hair, bangs feathered to the right, into the meeting room. Mike assumes the caseworker must need to join them and he nods in greeting.

"Dad?" Steve stands and takes two large steps before wrapping his arms around the man.

Mike's eyebrows lift and he tilts his head, taking in the strange sight.

The hell? Why is Steve hugging a stranger? Wait, is that Sam?

"Hi, Stevie. My, oh my, aren't you a sight for sore eyes." Strong arms hold the boy as tight as he can without causing pain. With closed eyes, he smiles through rotted teeth.

"Sam?" Stunned, Mike's jaw drops and he reminds himself that it's impolite to stare. "Holy shit. You look great. How are you?"

"I'm going to be okay, Mike. I can't thank you enough for bringing me here, little brother. I must have literally been out of my mind to live the way I did." Sam releases his son and motions for him to sit in the chair beside him.

"Steve. I don't know where to start." Tears stream down the cheeks of father and son. "That's not true. I've practiced this for two years. I am so, so incredibly sorry. I am so sorry, Stevie. I am so sorry."

Large, rough hands encase smooth smaller hands. "If I said those words every second for the rest of my life, it wouldn't be enough. I am so so so very sorry."

"I know, Dad. I'm glad you're better."

"Not yet, son, but with a lot of help, I will be. I have meetings every day to help me stay clean and sober. Saul and I speak every day, too. He's a great guy, Mike. I am incredibly thankful."

"Sam, I can't believe how far you've come in five short days. You look fantastic. I can't wait for the day we can spend hours and hours together, but today, we don't have much time. I don't want to cut this short, but we came to deliver some good news."

"Okay, what's your news, Mike?"

"You remember Gene? The traveling salesman who used to come into Red's?"

Sam nods.

"You know he left me his fortune. Well, come to find out, he is our uncle."

A shake of the head indicates that Sam doesn't understand.

"Grandpa Allen told me about a lady who he was with before he and grandma split up Well, as it turns out, she got pregnant and left town. He didn't know anything about it until years later. That person was Gene. He was Grandpa's illegitimate son. He was the millionaire who left me his entire fortune.

"Wow, Mike, that's great. Why is this such good news?" Amusement creates the same smile that Mike assumes Saul had on his face when he replied with the same answer.

"You haven't let me finish. There's more. Gene also left a large sum of money in a trust that has yet to be claimed."

With a nod to his nephew, Mike asks Steve to say the final words out loud.

"The name of the beneficiary is Samuel Higgenbottom. Dad, you inherited two million dollars."

Chapter 23

Brakes squeal to a halt behind the BMW and Mike cringes as he glances in the rear-view mirror. The school bus stops mere inches from his back bumper. Voices turn his attention to the double doors of the middle school as kids rush down the steps eager to break away from the classroom.

"Hey, I got your text. What's up?" Bells tied to the outside of Steve's backpack jingle as it bounces on the backseat. The front door closes behind Steve as he climbs into the passenger seat.

"Thought you might want to go with me to see your dad. He called and wanted to talk about his inheritance. He asked if I would bring you."

Sneakers, dirty from gym class, hold Steve's attention until he feels that his eyes are dry enough to meet Mike's.

"I'd like that." The toothy smile refuses to hide his

excitement. "I'm still worried about him, though. I hope that he remembers how good life was with us and how bad life was on the street. What if he goes back to his old ways?"

"That's a valid concern. We just have to stay involved, be here to support his good decisions, and pray for the best." Mike reaches over the console to pat his nephew's knee.

"And you know what? I bet he remembers how good life was with you every day. Even when he was at his lowest point, I bet he thought about you. Don't let that get in the way of you finding your way back to having a great relationship.

"It will take some time for your dad to heal, but he'll get there. He wants it bad enough to make it happen."

Steve nods his understanding.

To confirm, Mike throws in an "Okay?" and adds, "Don't be disappointed if things don't go the way you want them to, right away."

"You sound like Saul," Steve jokes and flashes a smirk.

"Smartass." Mike pretends to punch Steve's thigh as his knuckles meet jean material. "Hey, can you believe your dad already has an idea on how he can help his friends that are still on the street? I can't wait to hear what he's been thinking about."

∼

PAPERS COVER the table in the meeting room at Hope of East Tennessee and Sam stands against the wall, waiting for his company to arrive. After entering the room, Steve and Mike exchange glances with raised eyebrows and Steve shrugs.

Lists about rules and regulations and processes along with drawings of houses with flowerbeds and dogs are spread between Sam, Mike, and Steve.

"Boy, am I glad to see you." Outstretched arms reach for Steve and pull him close for a tight hug. Sam revels in the amount of joy the embrace from his son brings to his soul. He backs away and speaks a few lines that he rehearsed all night.

"I know I have a lot of work to do and a long road ahead of me, but please trust me when I say that I am ready to be a productive member of society again. And a dad, and a brother, and a son.

"I understand that what I did to you is absolutely reprehensible and will be unbearably difficult to forgive. I hope and pray that you find it in your heart to be patient with me.

"My first priority is getting clean. My second priority is making up for lost time with you so we can be a family again. I'll need your help." Sam glances at his brother to catch his gaze. "Both of you."

Steve smiles at his dad and Mike offers a nod and a wink.

"Look, I want to run something past you both." Pacing from one end of the table to the other,

Sam wrings his hands and gets right to the point. "I always thought there was a better way to be homeless. Yeah, I know that sounds weird but hear me out. The city doesn't do anything to help those that need it the most.

"There are so many people who want to get off the streets, but they just can't quite get there; there is always something stopping them. They end up giving up and falling into the life. Drugs and alcohol are a huge problem, but so is mental health. Now that I've lived it, I have an idea that I know will help.

"I want to invest my money into helping all my friends that can't help themselves. I want to buy a piece of land outside the city and put a bunch of little houses on it so at least there is a roof over their heads and a place to shower and keep food."

Mike and Steve exchange glances, mouths agape, and shrug.

"This is a stepping stone, not a hand-out or a life sentence. Once you have landed on your feet and are ready to get back into the world, someone else in need will take your place."

Unable to contain his thoughts, Sam goes into detail. "So, here's the thing, to be a part of this community, called Second Chances, you must either be actively looking for employment or have a job. Everyone that lives in the community has a responsibility in exchange for free rent. They have to want to get better; drugs and alcohol are strictly prohibited.

"They will work for their keep and obey all rules or risk eviction. We will have a counselor come in for AA and NA meetings and for overall guidance, like what Hope does for us, here."

Mike takes advantage of a brief pause to comment. "Sam, I love this idea. How long have you been thinking about a tiny-home community to help the homeless?" Palms flat on the table, Mike leans forward to get a better look at the drawings of the homes.

"I have been thinking of a way to convince you to invest in something like this from the first time I realized I needed help. I had totally forgotten about it for the last six months or so; I fell into the life.

"When I woke up last week and remembered that you came to see me, the ideas all flooded back, including the property name. You like? Now that I have the money, nothing can stop me.

"I will need your help, though. We'll need a chunk of land to start building. Could you do some hunting for me?"

"You got it, bro. And I love the name Second Chances; it's perfect. Of course, all this can only happen when you get better. I have faith in you, but the road isn't going to be easy. We can talk more about counseling later, but Steve and I are going to continue our weekly talks with Saul over Skype. I think you should plan on that, too, after your time here is done."

Mike moves closer to hug his big brother; the scent of Irish Spring is a welcome change. "What do you think you'll need? About ten acres?"

"That sounds about right. Oh, my God. I'm so freaking excited. I have so many details already hammered out. I know I just need to keep on the right track and stay clean. I know I can do it if you two are with me. And Mom." Tears fill Sam's eyes. "I can't express how much I hate the way I treated both of you."

Sam continues to convey his thoughts about the community. "One of the residents will be a groundskeeper to care for the lawns. Hopefully, James will be able to agree to the regulations. He used to be a stand-up guy and I think he would be a really great addition.

"Anyway, individuals can keep their own gardens, if they want. That would be their own responsibility. Flowers, vegetables, whatever. Wait. Mike," Sam pauses. "How are you going to help from California?"

FIREWOOD CRACKLES and flames flicker as Lisa tosses pillows on the floor in front of the fireplace. Mike's eyes focus on Lisa's sunset photo above the mantle.

"Pops painted this exact scene; the colors are so close it's creepy. I can't wait to show you the room my mom created as a kind of temple for my grand-ma. Every painting of her hangs on the walls and this scene is in the center of it all."

"Your mom is so great. Even after we broke up, she treated me like a part of the family. She's been amazing with Steve, so supportive and open to any ideas."

Supplemental heat emits into the living room to fend off the damp January day. Lisa invites Mike to join her on the floor and they stretch out and turn on their sides to face each other. Close enough that they can speak in low tones but not touch, they get comfortable.

Wine glasses remain empty on the coffee table next to a full bottle of red from the Parisian winery.

"Steve is so happy that his dad is getting better. His smile melts my heart." Mike tells Lisa. "You would never guess that Sam has an entire community planned already. I mean, he named the place and has thought about who he wants to have which responsibilities. It's unreal.

"His plans include a community center that can be used for get-togethers for residents only. If their families want to use it for other activities, there is a fee that will be donated to the maintenance of the community.

"Can you believe it? He's even planned what happens when the room is rented; the residents will have the activities outside. Games, scavenger hunts, kickball. He's changed into a completely different man in just a week. He's almost the brother I knew when I left for California, only better. Sober."

In no hurry to move from this spot or change the subject, Lisa lingers on each word. Mike's presence and the way he looks at her with passion in his eyes promises a positive playful future. Lisa envisions a life with Mike that not only offers the love she craves but humor, kindness, and generosity that not everyone is able to give.

"The map he made of the community is top-notch. He has planned for fifteen half-acre lots to allow for enough room to fence in the backyard for the residents to have a dog. But they can only have one, not two." Mike laughs and shakes his head.

"Sam will need to spend a lot of time in therapy working on getting back to normal, whatever that is. By the time he's ready to get back into the real world, at least a couple of the homes should be complete.

"I figure he'll need about ten acres. Sam said he's okay with spending about $500k and has asked me to invest the rest, except for enough for him to live on for a while.

"I haven't ever thought about tiny homes before. There's so much to learn. You want to come with me to check them out?"

Lisa is happy to lend her support and artistic eye. "Of

course, I do. I've seen a couple of them and have always been intrigued. Mike, have you heard about equine therapy? Like in "28 Days" with Sandra Bullock. It's been proven to help with addicts and mental illness. It works to alleviate mental, emotional, and physical symptoms and improve trust, confidence, and social skills."

With a tilt of his head, Mike signals for Lisa to continue.

"Horses are very sensitive to changes in energy, feelings. If someone is calm and their mind is at peace, the horse mirrors that emotion. When horses react to a patient, therapists can understand how the person is feeling, even if they can't see it through their emotions. It's fascinating, really."

"This is why I love you." A brief kiss lands on Lisa's lips. "Well, then, looks like we'll need to hunt for 20 acres. He'll need goats and chickens, too. What is that look? Why are you smiling like that?"

Lisa blinks slowly and smirks her response.

Mike's soft lips meet Lisa's at the same time his fingers thread into her long hair, pulling her face closer to his. The kiss intensifies and their hearts start to race in tandem with their breathing.

Passion almost overcomes the couple until Mike finds the strength to pause. There will be plenty of time to satisfy their hunger soon.

Very soon.

Mike kisses Lisa's nose and complements his

love. "God, you're incredible. You still drive me crazy. I could kiss you all night."

"I love to see you squirm." Lisa winks and plants another deep kiss on his lips.

A few seconds and a deep breath later, Mike opens his eyes and shakes his head.

Lisa changes the direction of the conversation. "You know, when I was at UT, I sincerely believed that I would get over you and find someone else to make me happy and spend the rest of my life with.

"It never happened. I couldn't forget you, the way you looked at me, the way you made me feel when you touched me."

Mike brushes her arm; his eyes follow warm fingers from her elbow to her shoulder.

"Yeah, like that. You never left my mind. Turns out the psychic I went to just after I started teaching was right."

Mike's eyebrows lift to join a smirk. "Really? What was her prediction?"

"She *predicted* that someone held a place in the back of my heart and he would reappear out of nowhere. The funny thing is, she said it would happen just after Christmas 2014. I laughed at her. Literally said "haha" in her face. She said: '*that man is the love of your life*' and that I should wait for him.

"Every date I went on after that, I compared to you. I could never bring myself to let anyone take up my quality time; I would fantasize about being with you. I love you, Mike. I can't tell you how happy I am that you're here."

A frown develops on Mike's face. "My only regret is that I didn't come home sooner. Things may be a lot different if I hadn't been so selfish."

Chapter 24
JANUARY 12, 2015

S andals in three different sizes sit next to a red and white plaid blanket spread over the grass in a local park. Picnic supplies include a wicker woven basket, a cooler, a frisbee, two baseball gloves, and a ball.

Children play Ring Around the Rosie with their mother in the distance. The sun shines bright in the sky and mountains rise in the background with a river winding past the park. Splotches of green and blue begin as paint on a brush and end as pine trees high on the hillside.

Happy little trees.

Allen smiles to himself as he channels the energy of Bob Ross. Reruns of the painter's episodes on PBS are a highlight of Centerfield's art program. An interpretation of Jan and Dominic's time with Anna, while

Allen's life changed for the worse in 'Nam, material-izes as happier days on the canvas.

"Beautiful, as always. You could make a million selling these paintings. They're fantastic." Bones of Allen's frail shoulder meet Mike's gentle grip. A frown follows his wide eyes and Lisa understands the sensation of a wilting man is not what Mike expects to feel.

"Your grandma wrote about days that she would take your uncle and mom to the park. I never witnessed it, but this is what I think it probably looked like. Your mom's favorite game was Ring Around the Rosie. She would spin around the living room all by herself singing the nursery rhyme before falling to the floor."

Mike moves chairs from along the wall to the space where Allen stands beside the easel. Lisa sits beside Mike and they listen while they observe another masterpiece coming to life.

"Laughter would spill over into the kitchen where your grandma made Dominic's favorite dinner, tuna noodle casserole and a strawberry Jell-o mold for dessert. God, I would have given anything to spend days like that with the kids. And Anna. My Anna.

"The day Dominic came into the world was the second-best day of my life. The first was the day Anna said, 'I do.' They were the reason I woke up in the morning, went to work every day, and spent every dime on food and rent. They were my whole life."

Mike squeezes Lisa's hand and she responds with a smile, tears in her eyes.

"The day your mother was born, I knew I had to be more, make more, give more. The military promised money for college and a better life after just two years of service. I was sold. I was going to learn electrical engineering and be successful. I was going to be the best father, husband, and friend that anyone ever knew.

"My dream was to spend the rest of my days watching my children grow and my wife smile and laugh. I was going to be at every ball game, school concert, and parent-teacher conference. That all changed when I went to war. Twenty-two years of mental tears..."

After Allen's eyes clear, he focuses on his grandson.

"I like when you visit, Mike. You give me a reason to remember the good. Who is your friend? Have we met?"

"Pops, this is Lisa. We dated in high school. Do you remember her from back then?"

"I knew you looked familiar. You're the love of Mike's life. That floozie he married in California never meant a thing to him, I promise you. I may have never met her, but I knew she wasn't right for you, Mike. Lisa is your match. Don't fuck it up this time."

Laughter erupts from the couple and Allen tilts his

head and raises his eyebrows.

"I won't, Pops. Promise."

"I mean it, Mikey; you better marry her before she comes to her senses. I know you can be a much better father than I ever was. The two of you will make the most beautiful babies."

BRICK PAVERS LEAD the way through a sea of green to the steps of a mansion built for a cotton broker in the early 1900s. Fine dining at Elizabeth on 37th in Savannah's historic district is sure to impress Lisa.

At least I hope it does. Danny, I've never been so happy. I think Lisa feels the same way I do. She said she loves me, so why am I second-guessing myself? I haven't been this insecure since I moved to Cali.

After our past, I can only pray she allows me to make up for lost time. You'll help me keep my word to Pops, right? You won't let me fuck it up, again? If I start to do something stupid, you'll kick my ass, right?

"Mike, you okay? You seem like you're somewhere else." Lisa's grip on Mike's forearm tightens.

"Yeah. Just talking to Danny." As if everyone on Earth talks to their dead friends, Mike responds without giving it a second thought.

A giggle from Lisa causes Mike's head to turn. "Oh. Yeah, that sounds weird, doesn't it? Well, it's the truth. Talking to him helps me relax; when he responds, it's like... What?"

The wind blows strands of hair off Lisa's shoulder. As she stands in the middle of the walkway, her hand finds Mike's. "Please don't take this the wrong way, but does he really respond? How can you tell?"

"He does. In his own way," Mike nods. "Thoughts enter my head that could only have come from him and I even hear his voice sometimes. I have smelled his cologne. It took me a while to get used to it, but it's true. I welcome it.

"After Dominic died, it doesn't happen as much. Danny's at peace, now, but I asked him to come back when I need him."

A kiss lands on his lips and Lisa's hands frame his cheeks. "That's beautiful, Mike."

ONCE THE COUPLE sits at their table, water, bread, and a bottle of house wine arrive. White linen tablecloths and original paintings enhance the first-class ambiance. True Savannah-style décor complete with deep red walls and hardwood floors set a perfect tone for Southern dining.

God damn, man.

"Danny's impressed with the restaurant," Mike smiles into the atmosphere.

Lisa tilts her head for a moment then offers a

warm smile as she reaches for Mike's hand. "I am, too. This house is absolutely gorgeous. I've never been to Savannah but have always been intrigued. Temperatures are different on the coast, I know, but eighty-two in January is absolutely divine.

"The history of this city is fascinating, too. Did you know General Oglethorpe, along with 120 passengers aboard the ship *Anne*, landed on a bluff along the Savannah River in February 1733? The thirteenth and final colony was named Georgia, and Savannah became its first city.

"Actually, it was the first planned city in the United States based on a grid system, allowing for wide streets and parks and squares. Twenty-two of the original twenty-four squares still exist.

"Oh, I could go on forever, but I won't bore you." Her eyes focus on the wine glass in front of her and she reaches for the stem.

"I love the sound of your voice, Lisa. It reminds me of home, of good people, of honesty, and respect. I could listen to you speak all night. Talk about something, anything."

"I want to hear more about you and Danny. Did y'all have a chance to spend much time together after you moved?"

"I would fly him out to California at least twice a year. Another week would be spent in some off-the-wall place. We would find any reason to go anywhere. One winter, we went to Banff to check out the true ski resorts.

"We spent a week in Paris two years ago. Spring is a beautiful time to explore all the wonderful scents of new growth and flowers mixed with freshly baked bread. It's unreal.

"Even though I have taken a dozen trips to Paris, each time the Eiffel Tower came into view, I would see your face and my heart would skip a beat," he finishes.

Mike touches Lisa's cheek and reaches for her hand. Lips brush her knuckles between each word. "Every. Single. Time. That's why I knew I had to take you there for New Year's Eve."

A warm smile shows Lisa's perfectly straight, white teeth. "Best trip ever."

"Remember how Gene used to talk about all the small towns he had the opportunity to visit? Oakdale being his favorite, of course. Danny and I spent a week in Bar Harbor, Maine and another in Eureka Springs, Arkansas. Small-town sight-seeing and bar hopping was the best way to relax and hang out.

"Gene, God rest his soul. I thank the Lord above every day that I was able to be in the presence of such a fantastic person."

Red wine touches Mike's lips and his eyes close as he revels in the flavor of oak and the faint scent of blackberry. When he opens his eyes, Mike finds Lisa staring at him. After a blink, she speaks.

"There is something that has been on my mind and I've tried to squash it, but..."

Eyebrows raise as Mike indicates he's listening and interested.

"Okay, I'll just spit it out. I have enjoyed every second with you. I have fallen in love with you again, but it concerns me that I may not be enough for you."

Mike opens his mouth as if to speak, but Lisa raises her hand. "Please let me say this. I'm just a country girl—a simple teacher with a simple life. I love my little house and my old Toyota.

"You're accustomed to so much glamour and glitz, I'm concerned that you'll have high expectations that I won't be able to meet. I'm not used to such expensive things, dressing the part, and jetting around the world."

"Lisa," Mike interjects. "You have nothing to worry about. Please believe me when I say that I love you for you, just the way you are. I have no expectations that you'll ever have to change."

After a deep sigh, Lisa puts a hand over her heart. "That makes me feel better." She squeezes Mike's hand and blows him a kiss.

"Okay, I have something to ask you then." Lisa sits forward. "Please don't think this is shallow of me, but I'm curious. How much did Gene leave you?"

Expressionless, Mike leans back in his chair. Straight-faced with an even tone of voice and calm demeanor, he tells Lisa, "Gene left me $250 million dollars."

Pursed lips and a nod are all Lisa can muster as she attempts to determine if Mike is being honest. "So, you're telling me that you're worth $250 million dollars? Wow. I don't know what to say. That's pretty intimidating."

"Well, no, Lisa. Actually, I'm worth closer to $500 million." A smirk appears as Mike glances at the empty wine glass—anywhere to avoid the gaping, wide eye, expression that covers the face of his love.

Lisa swears under her breath. "How..."

"I was able to rearrange the stocks where Gene had the majority of his money and they grew like a weed. Opening the bars was just fun at first, but then I fell into helping bands get signed. The first group had a contract written which included one percent of everything they made paid directly to me as a finder's fee. I didn't ask for it, but I didn't say no, either.

"That action paved the way for me to include it in the next forty bands contracts. Except Alli and Charlie. I refuse to take money from them."

With a grin, Lisa tells Mike, "You would never guess that you have that kind of money by spending time with you. Unless, of course, you stand next to the BMW or Gulfstream. How is it that having that kind of wealth hasn't changed you?" Honest curiosity reflects in her eyes.

"It did for a while. I thought I was King Shit for

the first year I was in L.A. All the parties, boozing, cars, yachts, jets. The physical things really don't make life better, just easier."

"What happened?"

"When I met Rebecca, she toned me down. She knew that I inherited my wealth and compared to her, I was out of control. She worked hard for every penny, then became a jerk. I was a jerk first, then learned to appreciate what I had. That was one of our many issues. Look, I'm sorry to bring her up..."

Lisa smiles and interrupts. "I asked. It's okay. Besides, your experiences make you who you are today. But I still don't understand why you decided to come home now."

"It was time," Mike nods. "Time to find my true self and to be with people that I love. After you and I split up, I never let myself fall in love again. My heart has always wanted to be with you. I just didn't know how. Until now."

Mike reaches into the breast pocket of his jacket and Lisa wonders why he's pulling out his wallet when they haven't eaten yet.

"I don't want to spend one more second without you. I never want to wake up without seeing your face next to mine. You complete the perfect package that I envision for my life. I love you with every beat of my heart, with every bone in my body, and every ounce of my soul."

Platinum molded into a small circle with a very

large princess cut diamond rests between Mike's fingers as he gazes at Lisa, waiting. She stares at the diamond before raising her eyes to meet Mike's.

"Lisa Marie Johnson, will you make me the happiest man alive and marry me?"

About the Author

KRISTI COPELAND is the author of contemporary and book club fiction. She lives in Texas with her husband and multiple critters on their ranch. When she's not writing, Kristi enjoys spending time with close friends, wine tasting, and cat collecting.

www.kristicopelandwriter.com

Look Out For

Oakdale Book 2

following Alli, Charlie, & Heaven Scent

COMING SOON